"How *do you* feel if I *kiss* you like this?"

When he'd reduced her to a formless lump of need and desire, Quint slowly raised his head. "Well?"

"Well, what?" He expected her to be able to think after he'd kissed her like that?

Quint smiled and raised his hand to brush a wisp of hair away from her face. "You're really something. It's too bad…"

Greeley had no trouble finishing his abandoned sentence. "Too bad I'm related to Fern," she said coolly. "You should have remembered my bad blood before you put on this exhibition for your employees."

"You kissed me back."

"Maybe I wanted to see what depths you'd sink to to get your own way. Letting everyone think you're interested in me when you're only interested in *using* me!"

D0048724

Dear Reader,

Sitting in my red-wallpapered office, I'm surrounded by family photographs. I love seeing my husband as a baby, my father as an adolescent and my daughter at age four holding her new baby brother.

For better or worse, we all have families. I didn't plan to write about the Lassiter family, but as one character formed in my mind I realized I was dealing with all three Lassiter sisters—Cheyenne, Allie and Greeley. Then their older brother demanded his story be told, and who can say no to a sexy man like Worth Lassiter? What started out as one book had suddenly become four.

I hope you enjoy reading about the Lassiter family and the strong men—and woman!—who match them.

Love

Jeanne Allan

Four weddings, one Colorado family

One Man to the Altar
Jeanne Allan

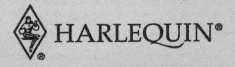

TORONTO • NEW YORK • LONDON
AMSTERDAM • PARIS • SYDNEY • HAMBURG
STOCKHOLM • ATHENS • TOKYO • MILAN • MADRID
PRAGUE • WARSAW • BUDAPEST • AUCKLAND

If you purchased this book without a cover you should be aware that this book is stolen property. It was reported as "unsold and destroyed" to the publisher, and neither the author nor the publisher has received any payment for this "stripped book."

ISBN 0-373-03584-5

ONE MAN TO THE ALTAR

First North American Publication 2000.

Copyright © 2000 by Barbara Blackman.

All rights reserved. Except for use In any review, the reproduction or utilization of this work in whole or in part in any form by any electronic, mechanical or other means, now known or hereafter invented, including xerography, photocopying and recording, or in any information storage or retrieval system, is forbidden without the written permission of the publisher, Harlequin Enterprises Limited, 225 Duncan Mill Road, Don Mills, Ontario, Canada M3B 3K9.

All characters in this book have no existence outside the imagination of the author and have no relation whatsoever to anyone bearing the same name or names. They are not even distantly inspired by any individual known or unknown to the author, and all incidents are pure invention.

This edition published by arrangement with Harlequin Books S.A.

® and TM are trademarks of the publisher. Trademarks indicated with ® are registered in the United States Patent and Trademark Office, the Canadian Trade Marks Office and in other countries.

Visit us at www.romance.net

Printed in U.S.A.

CHAPTER ONE

QUINT DAMIAN WANTED to jam the heel of his hand on the horn and blast away at the tourists crawling along Colorado Highway 82 in front of him. Sightseeing tourists. Just because they paid big bucks to visit a place like Aspen, they thought they owned the road. Why weren't they up in the mountains oohing and aahing at the dirty snow left over from winter? Flatland tourists acted as if a patch of unmelted snow in June was the eighth wonder of the world. They wouldn't think snow was such a wonderful thing if they'd ever had to haul a semi-trailer out of a twenty-foot drift.

Where was the turn off to the ranch? He didn't have all day.

He had two weeks.

Big Ed ought to have his head examined. Marrying a gold-digger like Fern Kelly. So much for the wisdom of seventy-six-year-olds.

Finally. The turn off. Scrambling up from the Roaring Fork River, his car clung tenaciously to sharp curves between looming red canyon walls before the dirt road spilled him out onto roller-coaster hills. Rows of barbed wire separated him from monotonous farm fields and pastures where demanding baby horses pestered their mothers.

Quint scowled impatiently at the gate on his right and tried not to think about the damage the gravel road was doing to his car. According to the directions given him by the woman at the St. Christopher Hotel in Aspen, this should be the place. A huge log arch with two touching circles burned into the top. The Double Nickel Ranch.

He forced himself to drive sedately through the gate. A small sign fastened to the gate read Hope Valley in faded paint. His mouth twisted cynically. Hope was for fools who waited for good things to come their way. Quint didn't believe in hope. He believed in going after what he wanted.

He wanted Greeley Lassiter.

Greeley heard the powerful engine long before the low, sleek black sports car glided arrogantly into the ranch yard. A distinct chill prickled her spine. It must be intense envy. Premonitions were for those with overactive imaginations.

The visitor stepped from the car. From her vantage point beneath the large pickup truck, Greeley could see only his sharply pressed charcoal-colored trousers.

Her mother had gone to Glenwood Springs, and her brother and the ranch hands were scattered about the ranch.

The legs strolled toward the ranch house. Shoes, similar to the expensive Italian loafers worn by Greeley's brother-in-law, raised slight clouds of dust across the yard.

Outside the shop, a honeybee droned around a clump of blue lupine. When she was five, Greeley had sat on her mother's lap without noticing a bee had landed there. She remembered the sharp pain when the bee stung her bottom.

A tiny whirlwind sent dust swirling into the shop and into her nostrils, threatening a sneeze. She pinched her nose with oil-stained fingers.

The uninvited visitor returned to his car. "Hello? Anyone around?"

The stranger's deep, masculine voice matched his sports car. Smooth, glossy tones with banked power. Confident. Self-assured to the point of arrogance. A friend of Greeley's insisted men drove expensive sports cars to compensate for sexual inadequacies.

This man didn't sound sexually inadequate.

Quint leaned against his car and inspected his surroundings. No one had come to the door of the old-fashioned, two-story, white frame house. The yard and barn appeared equally deserted, if one discounted several watchful horses in the corral and a huge barn cat whose eyes gleamed with animosity.

Coming to the ranch without phoning first had been a calculated risk. He'd wanted to see where Greeley Lassiter had been raised. A person's surroundings told a lot about her. He would have preferred a less prosperous-looking operation. A woman who needed money would be easier to persuade.

Cupping his hands to his mouth, Quint called again. A movement in one of the outbuildings caught his eye. Stretched out beside a large pickup, a black Labrador retriever raised his head, and feebly thumped his tail against a concrete floor.

Prepared to wait until some member of the Lassiter family showed up, Quint walked over to the Lab. Seeing the dog's white muzzle, he said, "You must be as old as Granddad. And have about as much sense. What if I'm here to steal the family silver?"

The ancient Lab sniffed at Quint's dangling hand, then laboriously rolled over on his back. Quint squatted down and scratched the dog's belly. "What is it with you old guys? Just because someone scratches your itch, you think he's okay?"

He saw the teenaged boy under the pickup as he started to straighten up. "Hello. I didn't see you under there. Didn't you hear me yell?"

"Yes."

Irritation flared, then Quint recalled his teenaged self had resented adults interrupting his activities for their own petty concerns. He gave the kid a commiserating smile. "But you hoped if you stayed quiet, I'd leave so you wouldn't have to deal with me."

The kid shrugged, letting his lack of hospitality speak for itself. Quint had no intention of leaving until he'd located his quarry. "I'm looking for Ms. Greeley Lassiter." The truck shadowed the boy, but Quint saw the teenager's eyes briefly flare in surprise.

After a moment the kid asked, "Why?"

Any sense of fellow feeling Quint had for the boy evaporated. "I'll tell her why, and if she wants to discuss it with adolescent males, that's up to her."

The boy stilled, his large eyes locked on Quint's face. Quint gazed steadily back. The teenager dropped his gaze and fiddled with the filthy baseball cap on his head. Finally he asked, "Who are you?"

"Quint Damian." Again the kid stared at him. Quint wondered if the youth was mentally slow. He had the high-pitched voice of a younger boy. "You didn't ask who Greeley Lassiter is, so I assume I'm at the correct place. Are you an employee of the ranch or a younger brother? I don't know much about Ms. Lassiter."

"Why should you?"

Reacting to the antagonism in the kid's voice would get him nowhere. Quint pinned a pleasant smile on his face. "An exchange of information, is that it? I tell you what you want to know, and then you'll tell me what I want to know?"

The kid gave him a narrow-eyed look. "Maybe."

Quint wanted to wring the teenager's neck. "We might start with your name." The kid remained silent so long, Quint felt like pulling him from under the truck and shaking answers out of him.

"Skeeter."

"You must not be one of the family."

The kid bristled. "Who told you that?"

"No one. I thought the Lassiter offspring were named after their father's rodeo victories."

"The Mesquite Championship Rodeo. Mesquite, Texas," the teen said defiantly.

Lying through his teeth, Quint thought. He gave the kid an incredulous look to let him know he wasn't buying the lie.

"A name like Quint's nothing to brag about either."

"No kidding." Quint had misread the teenager's tone.

With a name like Skeeter, the boy had probably been teased and hounded from the day he'd started school. Quint reluctantly identified with the kid's problem. "I had my share of fights growing up."

"Right." The kid obviously felt an adult couldn't possibly understand.

Quint saw nothing more to be gained by sticking around here. "I'm staying at the St. Christopher Hotel. Tell your sister to call me."

"Why?"

"Because I'm not a good person to cross."

The threat met with disdain. "I meant why should she call you?"

"Let's just say I have something of importance to discuss with her."

"Let's just say I want to know what."

"I'm sure you do." Standing, Quint brushed perfunctorily at his trousers. "I'm not leaving Aspen until I meet with her." He headed back to his car, adding insincerely over his shoulder, "Nice to meet you, Skeeter."

The kid didn't bother to answer.

Greeley watched Quint Damian stride arrogantly away. His thick, coal-black hair, dark, squared-off chin and resolute jaw gave him a tough, rugged appearance at odds with his sartorial elegance. Whoever he was and whatever he wanted with her, she wanted nothing to do with him.

He scared the living daylights out of her. Not because he'd warned her he wasn't a good person to cross, or because of the menace in his voice when he'd said it. Not because of the hard-muscled body she'd sensed under the swanky clothes or because of the way he'd loomed over her.

Because she instinctively knew he was bad news. A jay squawked an alarm from the cottonwood tree, and a shiver corkscrewed down Greeley's spine.

A car engine growled into the afternoon stillness, then the sports car leapt through the gate and disappeared.

For the time being. He said he wasn't leaving until he met her. Greeley discarded the usual reasons a stranger could be looking for her. Friend of a friend, potential client, male on the make. None fit Quint Damian.

She would not meet him.

He looked the persistent type—like the tiny spines on a prickly pear cactus which anchored in your skin, or a tick which burrowed into your flesh.

Quint drummed his fingers on the steering wheel, irritated he hadn't thought to offer the kid a bribe. Five or ten dollars to call Quint when Ms. Greeley Lassiter showed up. He snorted. This was Aspen, playground of millionaires. Around here, bribes probably started at a hundred dollars. Or more.

The town irritated him. The kid irritated him. The missing Greeley Lassiter irritated him. Even the bright June sunshine irritated him.

Most of all, his grandfather irritated him. Why Big Ed had hooked up with Fern Kelly defied Quint's utmost efforts to understand. He and the old man had been doing just fine for the past twelve-plus years.

Quint hoped no one expected him to call Fern "Grandma." An unholy glee seized him. Why not? Calling her "Grandma" was the last thing Fern wanted from a thirty-one-year-old man. Something to think about the next time Fern irritated him. Which occurred about every six seconds Quint was in her presence and almost as often when he wasn't.

The only good thing about this trip to Aspen was anticipating the look on Fern's face when Quint returned with his big surprise. One daughter dutifully delivered to Granddad's doorstep. Big Ed had swallowed hook, line and sinker Fern's Gothic tale of the baby wrenched from a mother's loving arms. Quint particularly liked the part about Fern being warned to never contact the child who'd been given to her lover's wife to raise.

He didn't believe a word of the story. If Fern had spent one second thinking about the child, whose name she apparently had trouble recalling, Quint would be amazed.

Fern had made a mistake when she'd mentioned the kid to Granddad in a bid for sympathy over her hard life. Big Ed had hired a private detective who'd easily located Fern's child. Quint had wanted to read the file which the private eye turned over to Granddad, but Big Ed, in one of those quirky spins of logic which Quint found both annoying and endearing, said snooping into a person's life wasn't right and claimed he'd told Quint all Quint needed to know.

Quint knew infuriatingly little. The name of the ranch. The name of Fern's lover—Beau Lassiter, now deceased and no longer a threat to Fern. Quint knew the reason for the odd names of the Lassiter offspring. He frowned. The detective had slipped up by missing Skeeter Lassiter.

Unless that was Granddad's doing. Granddad liked omitting a few relevant details when he gave Quint a problem to solve. Claimed it made Quint think harder, dig deeper and refuse to settle for easy answers.

A small jet roared low over the highway, startling Quint.

A thought came from nowhere to punch him in the stomach. Greeley Lassiter was the easy answer. Did that make her the wrong answer?

Greeley heard the phone ringing as she walked down the stairs.

Worth answered in the hall. "She's right here," he said and held out the phone.

Taking the phone from her brother, she spoke into it.

"Ms. Lassiter, my name's Quint Damian. I met Skeeter this afternoon and requested he ask you to call me."

She hadn't expected him to call. Not so soon. She thought he'd give her until tomorrow before he tried again to contact her. She thought she'd have time to figure out what he wanted and decide how to deal with him. Worth started to walk away, but he turned, giving her a curious look, her silence apparently striking him as odd. She had to say something. "I heard."

"You Lassiters are a friendly bunch, aren't you?" Quint Damian let the sarcastic question rest a minute before saying, "I'd like to meet you. At your convenience, of course."

"Why?"

"I'll be happy to explain when we meet."

The smooth evasion annoyed her. "Tell me now."

A long pause ensued. "Does the name Fern Kelly mean anything to you?" he finally asked.

Fern Kelly. Greeley had known for years exactly who Fern Kelly was. A woman who had slept with Beau Lassiter, given birth to a daughter, and then dumped the newborn baby on Mary Lassiter's doorstep. A baby Beau had named Greeley.

She hung up.

The phone immediately rang again.

Then rang three more times. The answering machine picked up, and Greeley's mother's voice informed one and all that no one could make it to the phone.

"Ms. Lassiter, I know you're there. I'd like to speak with you."

She imagined she could hear him breathing. Waiting to pounce.

"Ms. Lassiter, it would be to your advantage to talk to me."

Worth walked toward her, his eyebrows drawn together in a heavy frown. "What's going on? Some guy harassing you?"

"It's nothing. Ignore it."

Quint Damian's voice continued. "Obviously I shouldn't have mentioned your mother, but if you would meet me, I could explain. All I'm asking is that you listen to what I have to say."

"What about Mom? She's in the kitchen putting away groceries."

Greeley muted the answering machine, silencing Mr. Damian's voice in midword. "He wants to sell me something," she said, looking past Worth's shoulder.

"What?"

She scrambled for a credible answer. "A tombstone. For Mom. Said she's getting old."

Worth laughed. "I'd like to hear him say that to Mom."

"Say what to Mom?" Mary Lassiter walked into the hall.

"Some guy's trying to sell Greeley a tombstone for you because you're getting old."

"What?" Mary took one look at the red light blinking on the answering machine and snatched up the telephone. "This is Mary Lassiter, and I'll have you know I'm only fifty-three, and I don't expect my family to need a tombstone for me for a good thirty years or more, so you can just..." A stunned look crossed her face. "After all these years?" She stared at Greeley, her hand creeping to her throat.

Greeley abruptly sat on the chair beside the phone, her gaze locked on her mother's face.

"No, if Greeley doesn't want to speak with you, that's her business, I can't help you." Listening, Mary twisted the phone cord. "I don't know. Maybe I could drive in and meet you, Mr. Damian. If you explained it to me first?"

Dread cramped Greeley's stomach. "No." She grabbed the phone from her mother. "I'll take care of it." Into the receiver she said crisply, "Six o'clock. The Gilded Lily at the St. Christopher Hotel." She banged down the phone.

Worth looked from her to their mother. "Would someone please fill me in on what is going on?"

"I'm not sure," Mary said slowly. "A man named Quint Damian wants to talk to Greeley about Fern Kelly."

"Who's Fern Kelly? Oh. Her. What could she want with Greeley?"

"I have no idea. Do you, Greeley?"

Her mother and brother looked quizzically at her with matching blue eyes. Greeley's blue eyes had more of a gray cast, but she'd inherited the same cheekbones and mouth Worth had inherited from their father. "I wish I had blond hair," she blurted out.

Worth grinned. "You want to look like your bimbo sisters?"

"Yes."

Her brother's grin faded and he flashed his mother an enigmatic look.

"You inherited your glossy brown hair from your father." Mary reached over and trailed a thumb over one of Greeley's eyebrows. "That and your eyebrows. His hardly arched either."

"I don't have anybody's nose." Greeley meant her nose looked nothing like Worth's or her sisters'. Or Mary's.

"Sure you do." Worth draped his arm around her. "You have a little, pointy nose. Like the chipmunks out back."

"Creep." Smiling in spite of the block of ice in her chest, Greeley elbowed him in the side. "You know what I mean."

"I know." He gave her a quick squeeze. "I'll go talk to this guy. He can tell me what he wants."

Mary pressed a palm to the side of Greeley's face. "No, Worth. I should be the one to go. After all this time... I'll go see why Mr. Damian is here."

"We'll both go," Worth said.

Greeley wanted to let them. She couldn't. She'd taken advantage of their kindness and generosity for twenty-four years. Emotion clogged her throat. "I love you guys." Her voice sounded thick and weepy, and she swallowed hard. "I'm going, but thanks."

Worth eyed her steadily. "You don't have to, but if you're sure that's you want to do...."

"I'm sure." She'd never been less sure of anything in her entire life.

*   *   *

Everything about the quietly elegant restaurant told Quint he'd pay plenty for dinner at the Gilded Lily. Like mother, like daughter.

Greeley Lassiter was not among the few early diners. Although he'd never seen a photograph of her, Quint was betting he'd know Fern's daughter the instant he laid eyes on her.

A tall blond goddess with a glorious mass of sunlit hair walked into the restaurant. Her gaze roved around the room, lit on him and stopped.

Her undisguised interest puzzled him, until the answer almost knocked him off the chair. He hadn't expected Greeley Lassiter to be so tall. Or so blond. He would have bet his last dollar that Fern's blond hair came from a bottle.

He nodded. She gave him the kind of look women reserved for dog dirt on the bottoms of their shoes.

Ms. Lassiter was definitely unhappy about meeting him.

Quint pushed back his chair. Before he could rise, a young boy rushed in, followed by a tall, well-dressed gentleman, and the woman greeted them in such an intimate manner, Quint knew the three went together. The woman turned and Quint realized she was pregnant. Relaxing in his chair, he sipped his wine and watched the trio out of the corners of his eyes, mocking himself for egotistically imagining he in any way interested the woman.

Ms. Lassiter was late. Like her mother. Fern liked to make men wait. Quint smothered his annoyance. He'd wait as long as it took.

A small red-headed girl bounced into the dining room, greeting with glad cries the trio he watched. Even the boy submitted to the child's enthusiastic hugs and kisses. Her brother?

Quint had been an only child.

Another couple entered, a cowboy and a blond woman, who was a dead-ringer for the first woman except for her short hair.

He wondered who they were.

And why the obvious interest in him? Were solo male diners that unusual in Aspen? Annoyed by their intrusive scrutiny, Quint raised his wineglass in a salute.

Only the slightest narrowing of the second woman's eyes betrayed her displeasure.

The cowboy said something to her, and she looked over her shoulder. Quint followed her gaze and almost choked on his wine.

A brown-haired bombshell stood in the entrance, the bold, in-your-face red of her dress reverberating off the pale restaurant walls. There ought to be a law against sexy ankle-length dresses slit that far up the front.

Quint knew an insane urge to forget Greeley Lassiter and take this beauty straight upstairs to his hotel suite.

"Sir, would you care for something else while you're waiting?"

Quint started. Intent on the brunette, he hadn't seen the server approach. "No, thank you. I'll wait for my guest."

The server bowed away. He probably thought Quint had been stood up. Quint knew better. The carrot he'd dangled before Fern's daughter—the hint of money—would bring her here. In her own good time.

Reminding himself he needed Ms. Lassiter, he buried his impatience. The longer she dawdled, the longer he could watch the sex goddess. And fantasize.

He looked back toward the entrance. No one stood there. Ridiculously disappointed, Quint searched the room. She stood beside the table where the blond women sat.

Quint blinked. Maybe he ought to lay off the wine. Or spice up his social life. Granted, the woman was attractive, but hardly a sex goddess. With the red-headed child hugging her neck, the woman looked nothing out of the ordinary.

She turned and stared at him. The woman with the blond mane said something, but the brunette made a dismissive gesture, disengaged from the child, and walked toward Quint.

His gut clenched. What did she have, some kind of electronic sizzle button she hit when she wanted to up the voltage? If she upped it much more, he'd incinerate. Quint ignored the little voice reminding him he'd come here on business. He'd worry about Ms. Lassiter later.

The woman stopped at his table. "Mr. Damian?"

He stood. "Yes." Her flowery perfume made him lightheaded. Quint had no idea what was going on, but he was more than willing to let her set the pace. At first. After all, she'd gone to the trouble to find out who he was. Later, he'd find out everything he wanted to know about her. Anticipation tightened his muscles. He slowly smiled. "I know we haven't met. I wouldn't forget a woman like you."

She didn't return his smile. "I'm Greeley Lassiter."

"You can't be." The astonishment in his voice made him sound like a raw teenager. "I mean...you're not what I expected."

"You're exactly what I expected." She sat. "Your napkin fell to the floor when you stood so politely."

Cool sarcasm edged every word. She enjoyed knowing she'd knocked him for a loop. Great. He'd lost control of the situation before he'd started.

The server scurried over in response to a signal so subtle Quint almost missed it. "Mr. Damian would like a clean napkin," Greeley Lassiter said. "I'll have a glass of water."

"This wine is excellent." Quint intended to run this meeting. "May I pour you some?"

"No. Why did you want to meet with me?"

"Dinner first, then business." He tried another smile.

"I don't want dinner." She smiled at the server as he set a crystal goblet of water in front of her. "I'm not aware we have any business, Mr. Damian."

Her composed voice set his teeth on edge. For all the interest or emotion she displayed, they might be discussing the weather. He rejected the comparison. In Colorado, weather was an emotional subject.

Quint set his menu aside. "You probably want to know about Fern, I mean, your mother."

"No."

Ms. Lassiter was starting to irritate him. He couldn't decide if she was stupid, obtuse, or just plain rude. "All right. Let's talk about you."

She sipped her water. "Why?"

He should have known any daughter of Fern's would be a pain in the neck. "I thought a little polite conversation might be nice. I'm not checking your credentials or anything."

"I have no credentials, and I'm not interested in meaningless conversation." She pushed back her chair.

He would not let her make him lose his temper. "I'll get to the point then. As I told you on the phone, this will be well worth your time."

Her chair stayed back from the table, but she didn't walk away. "What would be worth my time?"

Well, he thought cynically. The mouse just went for the cheese. The only outcome to be expected from someone related to Fern. "Coming to Denver. As my grandfather wants you to do."

"Why does your grandfather want me to go to Denver?"

Grinding his teeth would solve nothing. She was dense as a brick. "I explained all that on the phone."

"I muted the sound."

Not so dense. The tinge of triumph in her voice told him she intended to annoy him. He refused to be manipulated into an argument she could use as an excuse to walk away. He needed her. Correction. He intended to use her. Folding his hands on the table, Quint strove to speak in a calm, patient voice. "Your mother plans to marry my grandfather."

"My mother has no plans to remarry."

"Remarry," Quint repeated in surprise. "I thought Fern had never married. Don't tell me she has an ex-husband she's never mentioned." Ms. Lassiter looked at him. Quint couldn't think of a woman of his acquaintance who would let a statement hang in the air without feeling the need to correct or amplify it. "Or did you think she married your father? It's my understanding he was still married to Mary Lassiter when he died."

"He was."

"So he couldn't have married Fern. Not legally." Illegal would be fine. Ammunition to use against Fern.

"Let me make one thing clear, Mr. Damian. My mother is Mary Lassiter. That other woman merely gave birth to me. I have no interest in her."

The curious lack of emotion rang false. Greeley Lassiter should be curious about her mother. Or want to spit in her face. Quint took a long, deliberate sip of wine. Making a decision, he set his wineglass on the table. "Fern told my grandfather you were forcibly taken from her and given to Mary Lassiter to raise."

Something flashed deep in her eyes before she said in a cool voice, "How tragic for her." His face must have betrayed his reaction because a crooked smile bent her mouth. "If I'm supposed to jump up and call her a liar, I'm afraid I can't. I don't remember my early days."

He couldn't believe how much he wanted to kiss Fern's daughter's bright red, mocking lips. Ruthlessly suppressing the suicidal urge, Quint said, "Granddad believes her story and he'd like you to come to Denver so he can give Fern what he believes to be her most passionate desire. A chance to be reunited with her baby."

"No." She took another swallow of water, set the glass on the table and made to rise.

"Wait. Please." Quint dragged his gaze from the workings of her throat and forced himself to concentrate on business. "At least let me explain the situation. Granddad is offering you substantial compensation for your time and effort. Are you sure you don't want something to eat or drink?"

"Yes."

He could use her on his side the next time he negotiated a contract. This woman gave nothing away. "You may have heard of Damian Trucking." He paused. She made no effort to fill the pause. "Guess not. Granddad started the business, expecting to leave it to his son, but my father was killed in Vietnam a month before I was born."

"I'm sorry." The first sign of a human emotion crossed her face. Sympathy.

Quint instantly rejected it. "I'm not asking for pity," he said curtly. "That's background. The point is, with no other children, Granddad raised me with the business. I've always known the trucking company would eventually be mine."

"I see. Now you're worried Fern might get it, so you want me to come to Denver and somehow queer the deal."

She'd gone straight to the core of the matter. A man would be wise to remember the pretty face hid a razor-sharp mind, and not get distracted by red dresses and gorgeous legs. "Although Granddad's been transferring ownership to me a little at time ever since I was born, to cut down on estate taxes and insure the company stayed in the family, he could only transfer a limited amount each year." In his opinion, the crippling inheritance tax heirs had to pay signaled the end of many a family business.

"Granddad still owns the lion's share of the company," Quint continued, "and in Colorado, surviving spouses inherit at least half their deceased spouse's estate. No will can change that. Fern's considerably younger than Granddad. I'll be frank with you, Ms. Lassiter, I don't think Fern and I could ever work together as partners." Talk about your classic understatement.

"That's your problem." She stood and walked away.

Only as far as the table across the room where the two blond women sat with the well-dressed man. The cowboy and the children had gone. If she sat with her back to him, hiding her face from him, he'd know she'd been putting on an act. She sat facing him. Demonstrating that Quint and his opinions were totally irrelevant to her. A server practically raced to her side. Greeley Lassiter was ordering dinner.

She gestured in his direction.

Like a remote-controlled toy car, the server moved to Quint's table. "Greeley said you're ready to order, sir."

"She own this place or something?" Quint snarled.

"No, sir. Not Greeley."

Annoyed he'd let her maddening behavior negatively influence him, Quint apologized to the server and ordered dinner.

Ms. Lassiter's meal arrived first. A hamburger and French fries. Quint knew neither was on the menu. She pulled at her fingers, removing gloves. He hadn't noticed she wore gloves. Admittedly, with that high slit skirt, he hadn't noticed much besides shapely, silk-clad thighs, calves and ankles. Ankles. Something about her ankles. Of course. They'd been crossed and clenched so tightly, it was a wonder she hadn't cut off circulation. Ms. Lassiter hadn't been nearly as indifferent as she'd pretended.

The game wasn't over. All he needed was the right incentive to persuade Ms. Lassiter to play. Watching her eat, he ran various possibilities through his mind.

She put down her sandwich, and the server scurried to her side, his body shading her face.

Quint snapped to attention. Something about the way the server's shadow darkened her pale skin triggered a sense of familiarity. An elusive memory teased him, and then it came to him. Squinting, he mentally added a baseball cap and a smear of grease on her cheek. Fury swept through him.

She'd played him for a fool from the start.

Brushing him off as if he were an insignificant fly.

Her mistake. No Damian ever gave up.

CHAPTER TWO

"HIS GRANDFATHER wants to marry Fern Kelly?" Allie asked. "I thought she was younger than Mom."

Greeley nodded to her sister. "That's why he's opposed. He's worried she'll outlive his granddaddy and inherit part of the family business he counted on owning."

"Colorado law," Thomas succinctly agreed. "Greeley, clarify something for me. You say he and his grandfather plan to surprise your mother—ouch!"

"Don't kick your husband, Cheyenne. It's your fault for doing other things..." she directed a meaningful look at her oldest sister's increasing midsection, "...instead of filling Thomas in on family history. Apparently the woman who gave birth to me knows nothing about their stupid plan."

The woman—no, the time had come to drop the ponderous identification and call her Fern. Fern obviously had no more desire to meet Greeley than Greeley did to meet Fern. Greeley had long ago accepted Fern's rejection.

A movement across the room caught her eye. Quint Damian stood by his table talking to his server and gesturing in their direction. Greeley chomped on a French fry as he walked toward them. The man had more nerve and arrogance than Worth's prize stallion. Strutted like him, too.

Mr. Damian stopped behind an empty chair and placed his bottle of wine and half-filled glass on the pink tablecloth before addressing everyone around the table. "I have a question."

Thomas, ever the gentleman, rose and extended his hand. "Greeley said you're Quint Damian of Damian Trucking. We've never met, but we've done some business. I'm Thomas Steele."

"Of Steele Hotels?" When Thomas nodded, the interloper gave Greeley a dark look and said, "That explains a few things."

Thomas chuckled. "Don't count on it." He introduced Cheyenne and Allie. "You've met my other sister-in-law, Greeley." Looking at the man's wine, Thomas added smoothly. "You'll join us, of course."

Greeley could have kicked her brother-in-law herself.

Thomas's unwelcome guest sat and looked from Cheyenne to Allie. "I'd never have guessed you're Ms. Lassiter's half-sisters."

"We're her sisters," Allie said.

"That woman in Denver is nothing to any of us," Cheyenne added coldly.

Warmed by her sisters' demonstration of loyalty, Greeley forced herself to continue eating.

"She's Ms. Lassiter's mother," Quint Damian said.

"Greeley has the same mom we do," Allie said firmly.

"Mary Lassiter." Cheyenne squeezed Greeley's thigh under the table.

Smiling as the older Lassiter sisters closed ranks against the outsider, Thomas gave Quint Damian a quizzical look. "You said you had a question."

"Is there a rodeo in Mesquite, Texas?" he asked.

Greeley choked on her hamburger, dropped the sandwich and thrust her hands under the table. Too late. His mocking eyebrows told her he'd seen the savaged nails and messy cuticles.

Cheyenne gave Greeley an odd look before saying, "The Mesquite Championship Rodeo. Beau, our father, started rodeoing there. Why do you ask about Mesquite?"

"Because of me." Greeley refused to let him disconcert her. "He saw me changing the oil in my pickup this afternoon and thought I was a teenaged boy, so I told him my name was Skeeter."

Thomas laughed. Cheyenne and Allie tried not to. Greeley worked on getting down her hamburger.

Emotional women irritated Quint, but Greeley Lassiter's unassailable calm went beyond mere irritation. The woman looked hotter than an overheated radiator, but frigid water ran in her veins. Kissing her would be like sucking on an ice cube.

So why did he want to?

The server placed a small plate holding an elegantly prepared Portobello mushroom in front of Quint. Quint welcomed the distraction. Ms. Lassiter might look like one sexy lady, but it would be fatal to his plan if he lost sight of who her mother was.

"Greeley, if you went to Denver, you could make the rounds of the art galleries," Steele's wife said.

Quint looked in surprise at his unexpected ally.

"I'm not going to Denver to meet her."

Cheyenne Lassiter Steele unconsciously touched her swollen stomach. "I understand it even less now."

By the merest coincidence, Quint happened to glance at Greeley Lassiter at the exact moment a flash of pain darkened her eyes. It disappeared so quickly he would have convinced himself he'd imagined it. And the quickly extinguished look of longing. Except her knuckles were white as she raised her glass to drink.

The water in her veins wasn't cold. It was hot and getting hotter, and one of these days the radiator was going to boil over.

Quint knew all about wanting something you couldn't have.

A decent man would leave Greeley Lassiter alone.

If she were anyone but Fern's daughter, he *would* leave her alone.

But Big Ed meant the world to him. Quint couldn't let

Fern destroy his grandfather. Tough as nails when it came to business, Big Ed believed in love.

Love hadn't saved two of Big Ed's babies or prevented his wife from dying in childbirth.

Love hadn't kept Big Ed's remaining child alive in Vietnam.

Big Ed couldn't count on love.

He could count on Quint.

Quint watched Greeley Lassiter calmly eat her dinner and toyed with the absurd conclusion that his mushroom had been hallucinogenic. Ms. Lassiter wouldn't know an emotion if she tripped over one. He didn't deserve the name Damian if he let misplaced compassion for Fern's daughter take precedence over his grandfather's welfare.

He directed his attention to her half-sisters. "All I'm asking is that she come to Denver for the next two weeks. Fern's already moved into the house, so Ms. Lassiter can stay with us. Since she'll have to take leave from work, naturally, we'll pay her for her time and for her expenses."

"I'm not going to Denver, Mr. Damian."

He looked directly at her. "Does family mean anything to you, Ms. Lassiter?"

"She's not my family."

"I'm thinking of my family. My grandfather can be a royal pain in the neck, but he worked hard to make his business a success. I can't let her destroy him or his life's work."

"His life's work? Or your inheritance?"

"This isn't about me."

"It's not about me. Thanks for dinner, Thomas. No, don't stand up. I'm gone."

Quint watched her out the door. She was going to be a tough nut to crack. The server set the main course in front of him. Quint had cracked tough nuts before. He picked up his fork.

"Well, Allie?" Cheyenne Steele asked. "Now what do you think?"

Allie Peters sighed. "You're right. I knew it the minute I saw the red dress. We have to convince her to go to Denver and meet Fern Kelly."

"You're on my side?" Quint asked.

The women gave him identical looks of disdain.

"We're on Greeley's side," Steele's wife said stiffly.

"You want her to go to Denver, I want her to go to Denver. I'd say we want the same thing."

Allie Peters said, "We want what's best for Greeley. You want what's best for you."

"We don't give a darn what you want," her sister added.

Steele gave him a wry look. "I know your reputation, Damian, and ordinarily, I'd put my money on you, but you're backing a losing hand when you bet against the Lassiter sisters."

She didn't hear the sports car drive up, and she didn't recognize the immaculate jeans and expensive running shoes, but Greeley didn't need to stand up and turn around to identify the unwelcome visitor walking up behind her. "Don't you have a life?"

"Big Ed and Damian Trucking are my life."

Greeley straightened and rubbed the middle of her back. "That's pathetic."

"What's this?" He asked, eying the piles of beat-up metal objects she'd moved from the small trailer.

She shot him a look of scorn. Even Davy, her eight-year-old nephew, recognized salvaged auto parts when he saw them. Quint Damian probably went through the full-service line at filling stations so he wouldn't dirty his hands pumping gas. Curiosity prompted her question. "Who's Big Ed?"

"My grandfather." He gingerly toed a cooling fan.

Taking off her wide-brimmed hat, Greeley removed a heavy work glove and wiped her forehead with the back of her hand. "You call your grandfather Big Ed?"

"Sometimes. I grew up hearing him called that. Give me

a pair of work gloves, and I'll help unload the rest of this junk.''

''Don't tell me you're willing to sacrifice your expensive jeans out of the generosity of your heart? Or would you expect a little favor from me in return? Such as a trip to Denver?'' She glared at him. ''I'm not stupid.''

''The jury's still out on that.''

Greeley looked at him in open-mouthed outrage before an appreciation of the absurd struck her. She uttered a derisive laugh. ''You're offering to move filthy car parts while you're wearing what looks like a silk shirt, and you're calling me stupid? Never mind. You probably have a dozen more in assorted colors.'' Or would they all be in the same shade of dark mossy green as his eyes?

''Why do you dislike me so much? Before you knew what I wanted, you pretended to be someone else.''

''I was alone, you were a stranger.'' Greeley shrugged. ''A woman has to be cautious.''

He shook his head. ''Your attitude had nothing to do with caution. You were downright rude.''

''Maybe your aura told me you were going to be a major pain in the neck.'' Averting her head, she concentrated on tugging her glove back on. He wanted the impossible from her, but it was more than that. Quint Damian irritated her. Like poison ivy.

Her answer silenced him for maybe ten seconds before he took off on another tangent. ''Were you happy here as a kid? Were they good to you?''

Greeley knew he didn't care. She didn't want him to care. Her life was none of his business. ''I slept in the barn and had to do every filthy job on the ranch. Satisfied?''

''I didn't mean—''

''Sure you did. You look at me and see a house sparrow in the nest.'' Stooping, she picked up a small section of crumpled fender, her fingers gripping the metal to the point of pain. "Two gorgeous blond sisters and brown little me."

"Is that how you see yourself?"

She'd ignored the question, leaping back up into the trailer, leaving Quint to speculate on what they used salvaged auto parts for on a ranch. A woman walking up cut short his speculations. Quint took one look at her blond hair and face and knew he was looking at Greeley Lassiter's stepmother. He gave her his best smile. "Mrs. Lassiter? I'm Quint Damian."

She silently studied him. Quint had a feeling that ten years from now she'd be able to describe every hair on his head, every wrinkle in his shirt, every smudge of dirt on his shoes. These Lassiter women worked at annoying a person. Hiding his irritation, he hung on to his smile, saying politely, "We spoke on the phone yesterday."

"I remember."

His smile slipped a notch at her cool voice. "Steele warned me about the other two. He didn't warn me about you."

"You know Thomas?" Mary Lassiter's demeanor underwent a lightning change at the mention of her son-in-law.

Quint almost claimed a life-long friendship with Steele, but reason stepped in, and he answered truthfully. "We met last night at the St. Christopher Hotel."

"I see." Her voice lost its warmth. "Why are you hassling my daughter?" She emphasized the last two words.

An emphasis not lost on Quint. "My grandfather wants to meet Fern's daughter. And bring about a joyful reunion of mother and daughter."

"Don't insult me, Mr. Damian. If Fern wants to see Greeley, all she has to do is come to the ranch."

"That's not what she told Granddad."

Mrs. Lassiter dismissed Fern's words with a contemptuous sniff. "Greeley's right. You want her to go to Denver and confront Fern in hopes your grandfather will turn away from Greeley's mother when he learns the truth."

Quint jumped as metal crashed to the ground behind him.

"She's not my mother." Greeley Lassiter stood at the end of the trailer, her stance as defiant as her tone of voice. Only her eyes betrayed her vulnerability.

She looked like a lost little girl, and Quint felt an irrational urge to take her in his arms and comfort her. He didn't know what it was about Greeley Lassiter that got under his skin, but whatever it was, he wanted no part of it. The woman was trouble in tight blue jeans. She'd be about as soft and cuddly in a man's arms as an eighteen-wheeler.

Now there was an assumption he wouldn't mind testing.

He'd like her in his arms. Without blue jeans or anything else. Was he insane? Was this the same Quint Damian who lectured his male employees on respect for women and ordered the pin-up calendar removed from the maintenance shop?

Greeley Lassiter would look more appealing draped naked over an engine block than Miss May had.

"Earth to Mr. Damian!" Greeley Lassiter waved a piece of rusted tailpipe at him.

"What?"

"Go home. I am not going to Denver. I have no interest in seeing that woman."

The loud, precise way she spoke brought back an ancient memory. Granddad telling him, at six or seven, that a huge mutt who had terrorized Quint would leave the young boy alone if Quint showed no fear. Quint had faced the dog, and spoken with the same outward blustery bravado. All the while inwardly quaking like aspen leaves.

He wondered if Greeley Lassiter's cool intransigence signified disinterest or fear. He bet on fear. "You're afraid to meet your mother."

"I'm not afraid and she's not my mother."

Out of the corners of his eyes, Quint saw Mrs. Lassiter spring to attention. "You're afraid," he repeated with growing conviction. "Why? Fern can't do anything to you."

"I'm not afraid of her."

Something bumped his knee. Quint glanced down to see the ancient black Lab gazing expectantly at him. Wondering how he could use her fear to gain his ends, Quint absently leaned down and scratched the dog behind his ears. "Hey, old fellow, how you doing?"

"Don't waste your time trying to soften me up by pretending you like dogs. He's not my dog."

"What would soften you up, Ms. Lassiter?"

"Nothing. I'm rock-hard through and through. I don't care if your grandfather is going to die or—"

"He is, of course."

Remorse immediately covered her face. "I'm sorry. I didn't know. I mean...I meant, when he died and left the business...I shouldn't have said...I'm so sorry."

If he had less scruples, he'd use her guilt against her. Cursing an inconvenient conscience, Quint said with a crooked grin, "He's going to die some day. Nobody lives forever."

"That was despicable."

"He'll like you." The minute he said the words, Quint knew they were true. Granddad would be crazy about Greeley Lassiter.

But then, he was crazy about Fern.

"We'll never know, because he's not going to meet me."

"When I was a kid, he used to send me to the bakery for hard rolls."

She made a face. "A charming bit of nostalgia."

"You remind me of those hard rolls."

"Women must stand in line to receive your compliments."

"You ever had a hard roll fresh from the bakery? They're rock hard on the outside," he gave her a mocking smile, "and soft as a pillow on the inside."

He'd forgotten about her stepmother until Mary Lassiter stirred at his side. "There's a lightweight chair on the porch, Mr. Damian. If you're going to watch Greeley work, you'll be more comfortable sitting."

*   *   *

The hot sun did nothing to cool Greeley's temper. She hauled a crumpled bumper from the trailer and tossed it on a pile with other bumpers. Quint Damian had been quick to take advantage of Mary Lassiter's ingrained sense of Western hospitality.

"Sure is a beautiful day. Blue sky. Puffy white clouds. What's that big bird flying around in circles up there?"

Greeley fanned herself with her hat and looked at the turkey vulture riding the currents. "Buzzard. Since you haven't moved in over an hour, he probably thinks you're some kind of dead vermin." In case he missed the point, she added, "As opposed to live vermin."

Lounging in a chair in the shade of the cottonwood, Quint Damian acknowledged the insult with a wave of his glass of iced tea. "The chocolate cake your stepmother brought out was delicious. You should have had some. Might have sweetened you up." When she didn't respond, he closed his eyes and shifted his feet to a more comfortable position on the trailer's back bumper. "Tell me about your father. I can't get a handle on him."

"Beau was Beau." A rodeo cowboy with too much charm and too little dependability, he was notorious for his playing around. Greeley often wondered if Beau had fathered other bastard children. Children whose birth mothers hadn't discarded them.

"That doesn't tell me anything." Quint Damian opened one eye. "Mary Lassiter and Fern Kelly couldn't be more different. How'd Mary fall for a guy who'd go for Fern?"

That Quint Damian and her mother had reached a first-name basis with each other was only one of the thousands of things about him which annoyed Greeley. "None of your business."

"Sex, I'll bet," he said sagely.

"It was not." She hated the way he lifted an eyebrow at her vehement disagreement. The eyebrow stayed up, waiting. Maybe if she answered him, he'd take those darned black eyebrows and go away. "Mom fell for his smile. She said Beau could charm the birds out of trees when he smiled." Greeley had never understood how her mother could have found a smile so bewitching. Worth had a beautiful smile— Beau's smile, her mother claimed. Greeley's stomach didn't turn flip-flops when Worth smiled.

"Did you fall for his smile?"

"When I was four, I climbed that old cottonwood and couldn't get down. I told Beau to smile me down."

"Did he?"

"His arm was broken," she said curtly. "My brother climbed up after me." The incident had taught her the futility of relying on a man's charming smile. Shoving Quint Damian's feet out of her way, she picked up the broom to sweep the trailer floor.

"Were you scared?"

"Why do you bother to ask? You've made up your mind I'm the biggest coward who ever lived."

"You could change my mind."

"The only thing about you I'm interested in changing is your present location."

"Steele told me you're stubborn."

"You should listen to Thomas." She vigorously swept the trailer. It wasn't her fault he sat directly in her path.

"My mother," he loudly sneezed, "claims I'm pretty stubborn myself."

Greeley leaned on her broom handle. "You don't have a mother. People like you crawl out from under rocks."

"You didn't get that sharp tongue from Fern. Butter wouldn't melt in her mouth."

"I didn't get anything from her." He could take that any way he wanted.

"You have her nose. Thin, and kind of pointed. I've always thought Fern needs a broomstick to go with her nose."

"Isn't it lucky I have one to go with mine?" She resumed her sweeping.

He hastily moved his chair. "The nose works on your face."

Before Greeley could decide how to interpret his remark, Allie's sports utility vehicle drove through the gate.

Quint Damian followed the direction of her gaze. "Looks like one of your half-sisters."

"Sister." Quint Damian wasn't listening. He was watching the oncoming car with an odd expression on his face. It took her a moment to decipher it. Quint Damian practically quivered with the same air of expectancy Shadow exhibited when he saw a nice, juicy bone coming his way. "She's married."

"What?"

Hitting him over the head with the broom would probably hurt the broom. "Allie's married," Greeley said curtly. Jumping out of the trailer, she went to meet Allie and Hannah. Quint Damian's abstracted air told a familiar story. When Cheyenne or Allie appeared on the scene, men forgot Greeley's existence. Which was fine with her.

Greeley couldn't think of anything she wanted more than for Quint Damian to forget she existed.

Allie Peters and Cheyenne Steele had refused to discuss with him what they intended to do about Greeley Lassiter meeting her real mother. Quint suspected Allie Peters's trip to the ranch was the first step in their plan.

She'd brought a kitten as a reason for her visit. The red-haired child carefully carried the animal, so proud of being entrusted with the responsibility, Quint had trouble not laughing. Uninvited, he trailed them into the house, where the tiny, gray-striped feline ended up in his lap. Explaining he didn't care for cats didn't seem too smart right now.

"Somebody 'bandoned three of 'em," the child explained. "Mama said it wouldn't be fair if we got to keep them all, so you get this one, Grandma Mary."

A mouse-colored greyhound considered Quint from across the room. Quint stared back and hoped he'd get the feeling back in his foot once the sleeping black Lab woke up and moved his head.

Allie Peters looked at the kitten. "Some people think you can tell a lot about a person when you see them with animals."

"I wouldn't put much stock in that theory."

"I don't, Mr. Damian."

Quint smiled at her. "Your mother's agreed to call me Quint. I wish you would, too."

She hesitated before agreeing. "All right. I'm Allie."

"It's not that animals like him," Greeley Lassiter said. "They know they don't have to worry about him moving. Unless someone offers him a more comfortable chair."

Allie ignored her half-sister's tart interjection. "Do you have animals?"

"A dog I picked up at the pound. Granddad wanted a guard dog for the business."

"I suppose you turn him loose at night to bark and growl at passing strangers," Greeley Lassiter said contemptuously.

Quint looked down at the sleeping kitten. "No."

"Guard dogs need to be well-trained so they don't become aggressive," Allie added.

"He went to obedience school."

The Peters child draped herself over the arm of Quint's chair and gently smoothed the kitten's fur with a finger. "Did you know that kittens grow in their mama's tummy?"

"Hannah, honey, he doesn't want a lesson in biology. She's currently fascinated with babies," Allie explained.

"I'm just going to tell him about Aunt Cheyenne." Hannah looked up at Quint. "Did you know she has a baby in her tummy?"

"Well, actually, yes, I noticed."

"She's getting fat." The child swung around. "Were you fat when Uncle Worth lived in your tummy, Grandma Mary?"

"Big as a house," her grandmother answered cheerfully.

Hannah turned back to Quint. "I don't see how Uncle Worth fit, do you?"

The child's female relatives gave no signs of rescuing him. Obviously they enjoyed watching him squirm. "I, ah, don't know your Uncle Worth."

"He's big, like you. Mama and Aunt Cheyenne grew in Grandma Mary's stomach, too, but Aunt Greeley didn't. Mama told Daddy a lady dumped her on Grandma Mary's porch. Like the kittens."

The three women practically sucked all the air from the room with their sharp, indrawn breaths.

Quint smothered a tiny spark of compassion. He wasn't planning to hurt Greeley Lassiter. The woman was an adult. It wasn't as if she didn't know she had a loser for a mother. He was offering her money. All she had to do was go up to Denver, spit in her mother's eye, and come back to Aspen. She had nothing to lose but time, and he'd pay her for that.

She was playing hard to get—to up her price.

"That's not exactly what I said, and even if I had, you're not supposed to repeat things you hear," Allie said.

The child wrinkled her brow. It was apparent Hannah had a question she badly wanted to ask, but she couldn't decide if the question violated the rules. Quint sensed the women praying she'd hold her tongue. Silently he urged the child on. He needed every bit of information he could dig up.

Greeley Lassiter spoke first, in a rush of words. "How's Hannah's paint horse coming along, Allie?"

"She's a dream. Smart, and full of cow sense. She—"

"How come the lady dumped Aunt Greeley on your porch, Grandma Mary?" The child's curiosity prevailed.

"You misunderstood what you heard, Hannah," Mary Lassiter said firmly. "The lady gave Greeley to me. Your aunt was a very, very special present."

"Like the kitten?"

"More special. I had a brand-new daughter."

"Like I got a new mama and Mama got me when my mommy went to Heaven and Mama married my daddy?"

"Yes," her grandmother said. "Allie's your mama now and she loves you very much, and I love Greeley very much. And I love her sisters and brother and you and your cousin Davy and your daddies."

"I love Aunt Greeley, too," the child said loyally. "So does Davy, 'cause she lets him ride on the tractor, but I love her because she makes beautiful horses." She looked at Quint. "Do you love her?"

No wonder Fern had never wanted kids. He thought fast. "I've never seen her horses."

"I'll show you."

"He doesn't want to see them."

About to refuse the child's offer, Greeley Lassiter's quick objection changed Quint's mind. "There's nothing I'd rather see." He smiled at Ms. Lassiter.

She bared her teeth in a caricature of a smile.

Greeley couldn't decide which infuriated her more, the way Quint Damian manipulated her mother and sister with his sexy smiles, or the way Allie flirted with him, practically simpering when she told him to call her Allie. Allie was a little old to be flirting. Not to mention a little too married.

As for the man strolling along ahead of her, he was so arrogant and self-centered, he made her hair hurt. Greeley wanted him to go away. She didn't care if he did look like Hollywood's idea of a young, successful business tycoon, he couldn't come to Hope Valley and tear apart her carefully constructed world, for no other reason than that he wanted his own way.

At least he wasn't interrogating her niece on the details of Greeley's life as Hannah skipped at his side, swinging their clasped hands and chattering a mile a minute. Not that he hadn't filed away every little tidbit he'd already gleaned from her family. Filed them away to use against her.

Her mother and Allie had declined to join the excursion to Greeley's shop out back. Greeley knew why. They wanted to discuss her and Fern Kelly. They ought to be discussing ways to get rid of Quint Damian. They couldn't possibly think Greeley had the slightest interest in seeing a woman who meant nothing to her.

Hannah commanded Mr. Damian to shut his eyes. Greeley hoped he tripped over a blade of grass and fell flat on his face.

"Aunt Greeley made Daddy and Mama shut their eyes before they could see our horses."

"They're shut." Quint Damian held his arms out straight. "Lead on."

Hannah giggled and pulled his hand. "This way." She led him around to the back of Greeley's workshop. "Look."

He said nothing as he stared at the completed statue.

"You have to squint," Hannah said knowledgeably. "And pretend you're a horse."

He still said nothing. Greeley assumed he was squinting. She assumed pretending he was a horse was beyond him. He probably couldn't think of anything polite to say. Except why he'd bother to be polite now was beyond her. A polite person would have accepted "no" as final and left her alone.

"Do you make anything besides horses?" he asked finally. "Could you do something like this, only representing long-haul trucking?"

"Very funny." His mocking her sculpture didn't hurt one bit. His idea of art was probably naked women painted on black velvet.

"If you came up with something like this relating to trucks, I'd buy it in a minute," he said in a preoccupied voice, walking around the sculpture, studying it from all angles. "Incredible. Using junk, you've managed to convey power, movement, speed...."

She knew insincerity when she heard it. Hiding her anger, Greeley played along. She suspected this man did nothing without a purpose. She might as well find out what he was plotting now. "Why long-haul trucking?"

"I told you last night. The family business. Damian Trucking."

"Very clever. You commission a piece from me, and then, oh, so incidentally, you want me to deliver it to Denver. And coincidence of coincidences, I'll come face to face with the woman who gave birth to me. Would you expect me to cry out in horror, point my finger at her and call her a witch or something? What would make your grandfather banish her from his life?"

"One has nothing to do with the other. I'll drive over and pick it up myself."

"And quit bugging me to go to Denver?"

"As I said, one has nothing to do with the other."

"Look, Aunt Greeley! A big butterfly."

Greeley turned to see her niece chasing a large yellow-and-black swallowtail. The butterfly landed on a pile of crumpled bumpers. "Stay away from there, honey. That pile isn't very stable."

Ignoring her aunt's warning, Hannah stepped on a wobbly bumper and reached toward the butterfly. Greeley moved quickly toward her niece.

The butterfly flitted away before Hannah's outstretched hand touched him. Hannah stamped her foot in frustration. The clash of falling metal sounded simultaneously with the child's startled cry.

Quint Damian dashed past Greeley and with one arm swept Hannah out of danger. With his other, he blocked the falling automobile parts. Greeley released her pent-up breath as he set her niece safely on the ground.

Her relief was premature. Between them, Hannah and Quint Damian had disturbed the delicate balance of the unwieldy pile, setting off a chain reaction. Greeley watched in horror as an old crankshaft landed on the extreme end of a bumper causing the other end to flip another bumper, which catapulted an old hub cap through the air. The hub cap bounced off Quint Damian's head. Blood welled up and ran down the side of his face.

"Don't touch it," Greeley said sharply. "You'll make it worse." She dug a clean tissue from her pocket and pressed it against the wound. "It probably bled enough to flush out any dirt, but you'd better come inside so I can wash it, just in case. I picked that hub cap up at a junkyard. Hannah, run tell Grandma Mary what happened."

"I'm fine." He brushed aside her hand. "Don't fuss." Blood streamed down his face.

"Quit acting like some stupid tough guy. Of all the dumb klutzes...why didn't you watch where you were going? Now I'll have to take you to the hospital."

"I'm not going to the hospital."

Greeley Lassiter drove as if she and the car were a single, well-oiled machine. Quint pressed a clean washcloth to his cut. "The only reason you're insisting on this charade of taking me to the hospital is because you want to drive my car." If he hadn't lost so much blood, he wouldn't have lost the argument about her getting behind the wheel.

"You're grumpy because if I'd driven you in my pickup, your car would be at the ranch, and you'd have an excuse to return."

"I'm not grumpy and I don't allow women to drive my car." If his head hadn't hurt so badly, he'd never have given her the opening.

Naturally, she exploited it. "How chauvinistic. I suppose you think women shouldn't even be allowed on the road?"

"We have women truck drivers," he said defensively. "A number of our drivers drive as a team with their wives."

"I suppose the men take the little women along so they'll have someone to reach in the cooler and hand them a soda pop?"

"Their division of labor is up to them," he said stiffly.

"Head hurt pretty bad?"

"No. And if you had an ounce of compassion you wouldn't harass me while it does."

"We're almost there," she said in a soothing voice. As if he were her niece's age.

"I don't want to go to the hospital."

They turned off the highway. "I'm not ignoring a cut that close to your eye."

"I'm not going."

"Don't you hate it when someone insists you do something you have no intention of doing?"

"The situations have nothing in common." He removed the washcloth from his face as she pulled into a parking lot next to a low, brick building. "The bleeding has stopped." Blood ran from the cut. He slapped the cloth back to his face, wincing at the pain.

Greeley turned off the engine and stepped out of the car. He stared straight ahead. She couldn't make him get out.

Opening his door, she said, "You walking in, or do I have to go fetch men with a stretcher?"

Giving her a dirty look, he slammed out of the car.

A short while later, he breathed a sigh of relief. After a painfully thorough cleaning, the doctor had closed the cut with glue. Quint started to stand.

"A tetanus booster and then you're done."

"I don't need a shot," Quint said hastily.

"Maybe not, but with filthy, rusty metal, no point in taking any chances."

A nurse walked into the room. Quint took one look at the elephant-sized needle and the room went black.

"Go ahead, say it before you explode and hurt yourself," Quint Damian said savagely from his supine position on the couch in his hotel suite. "I'm sure you found the whole episode highly amusing."

She had, but fortunately he'd been out cold when she'd

been unable to keep from laughing. Remembering how he'd been injured, Greeley said in a conciliatory voice, "There's nothing to say. We all have our little guilty secrets."

"It's not a guilty secret," he practically shouted. "I don't like needles, okay? Lots of people don't like them."

"I'm not crazy about them myself, but I don't take one look at them and hit the floor so hard half the people along the Roaring Fork River think we're having an earthquake."

"I thought you had nothing to say. Go home."

"The doctor said I should keep an eye on you, in case of concussion. Want another pillow? Something to drink?"

"No, and quit fidgeting. I'm not going to sue you, if that's what you're worried about."

"That never entered my mind."

"What then?"

"What makes you think I'm worried about anything?" she asked evasively. The man was supposed to have a head injury. He had no business thinking he could read her mind.

"You've been giving me all these sideways glances ever since we got back to the St. Christopher. Whatever's on your mind, spit it out."

"All right." Crossing her arms across her chest, she glared down at him. "This doesn't make any difference, so don't think it does. I'm grateful you rescued Hannah, and I'm sorry you cut your head, but I do not feel obligated to go to Denver."

"Your gracious thanks are accepted," he said sarcastically. He closed his eyes. "Now go away."

Greeley bit one side of her bottom lip. Was it her imagination or was his face devoid of all color? Filthy, lethal germs could have covered the hub cap. Infection might already be raging in his blood stream. Kneeling quietly beside the couch, she gently touched the side of his face with her hand. Beard stubble rasped against her palm. His cheek felt warm, but not feverish. Succumbing to an idiotic urge, she lightly traced the hard line of his jaw with her thumb.

"When I was little and hurt myself," he said, "my mother would kiss my injury to make it better."

CHAPTER THREE

GREELEY INHALED SHARPLY as Quint Damian captured her hand and lightly kissed the sensitive palm. "I'm not your mother."

Opening his eyes, he smiled slightly, a sexy little movement of lips which made her insides dip. "I know," he said. "I'd rather you kissed my mouth."

She'd never seen anyone with irises that particular shade of green. A cool gray-green. Only not so cool, as warm currents of an emotion she couldn't identify swirled around black pupils.

Quint Damian must have a concussion. Worse, his concussion was contagious. There could be no other explanation for her wanting to kiss him. The whole idea was insane. Or the aftermath of a stressful afternoon. "Your injury's making you delirious."

"Probably."

"I can't think of any other reason why you'd want me to kiss you. Unless..." She eyed him suspiciously. "I suppose this is another ploy to get me to go to Denver?"

"No. It's an urge to satisfy an overpowering curiosity." Still holding her hand, he toyed with her fingers.

Not that she couldn't break away. She could. And would. In a minute. "Curiosity about what?"

"Your mouth. You're a woman of many disguises, but you can't disguise your mouth."

"It's Beau's mouth. We all have it."

He shook his head and winced. "It's your mouth, and I want to taste it."

Quint Damian had been injured. His wince proved his head hurt. He should be humored. A simple, little kiss meant nothing. She was twenty-four years old. It wouldn't be her first kiss.

Curiosity ran both ways. What kind of kisses did a man with such a firm mouth give? Cold, hard kisses? Selfish, inflexible, dominating kisses? She could always pull away. Worth had taught her a thing or two about defending herself against aggressive men.

No sign of impatience showed on Quint Damian's face. He simply waited. As if confident of the outcome.

Greeley stalled. "Do you really think your cut will feel better if I kiss you?"

"No."

If he'd said yes, she wouldn't have kissed him. Slowly leaning down, she rested her mouth on his and closed her eyes.

He made no move to pull her to him. At first his mouth remained perfectly still, then his lips touched hers in a kiss as soft as the wings of a yellow butterfly. He skimmed his mouth over hers before gently drawing her lower lip into his mouth and running his tongue between her parted lips.

Sensation rocketed through Greeley. Tasting the orange juice she'd made him drink when they'd returned to St. Chris's, she knew orange juice would be forever joined in her mind with kissing Quint Damian.

Her breathing quickened, bringing to her his scent, a heady, seductive blend of fragrances—woody, sensual, masculine, and clean, with the barest antiseptic edge. Warmth traveled between their bodies, curling her toes.

He hadn't locked his arms around her. He didn't hold her in any way. She could stop kissing him any time she wanted.

Her arm lay between them with his hand curved around hers. Her breast rested on his hand. Quint Damian moved his fingers slightly. Enough to allow the tip of her breast to slip between two of his fingers. Her chambray shirt provided no barrier to fingers which gently investigated the hard, sensitive nub. An erotic pressure grew deep in the center of her.

Making her greedy for more.

Quint Damian stopped kissing her.

One second his mouth slanted warmly over hers, the next second, empty air chilled her abandoned lips. With great effort Greeley controlled her breathing as he removed his hand from between their bodies.

"Is your curiosity satisfied now, Mr. Damian?" She forced a bright tone to her voice as she sprang to her feet. Her shaking knees came close to embarrassing her.

"I think we've advanced beyond the Mr. and Ms. stage, Greeley. Call me Quint."

To his amazement, Greeley hadn't argued. She hadn't called him Quint either.

Or mentioned their kiss. Or ripped off his clothes and lustfully attacked him.

Or run away.

She'd given him a history lesson on the origins of Aspen.

He now knew more than he'd ever wanted to know about silver mining in the late 1800s and the town's rejuvenation in the 1930s with the onset of skiing.

He knew much less than he wanted to know about Greeley Lassiter.

After she'd exhaustively covered Aspen's history, Greeley had lectured extensively on the cultural opportunities in Aspen, covering the art museum, the jazz festivals, and the various musical and educational events which took place during the summer. Then she'd abruptly declared he obviously didn't have a concussion.

Within seconds, taking advantage of her status as half-sister to the owner's wife, she'd arranged for one of the hotel's vans to drive her to the Double Nickel Ranch and scurried out the door as if the hounds of hell were in hot pursuit.

Leaving Quint to berate himself for his crazy, inexplicable behavior—kissing Fern's daughter. Had he lost his mind?

Worse, knowing the kiss had been a huge mistake, he'd wanted to kiss her again. He'd wanted her to stay. All night.

Loss of blood. Light-headedness from the sight of the needle. Reaction from the anti-tetanus serum or whatever they'd shot into him. Maybe he'd sniffed the stuff they'd used to glue his skin together and poisoned his brain. Pay your money, sucker, and take your pick.

He knew one thing with absolute certitude. He had no business kissing Greeley Lassiter. Much less wondering what she'd be like in bed.

Her mother's kiss had done nothing to arouse him.

Fern Kelly's daughter. He'd known she'd be trouble.

He simply hadn't realized how many guises trouble could come in. So far Greeley had masqueraded as a teenaged mechanic, a luscious siren in a red dress, and an artist who turned piles of junk into powerful statements. Not to mention a doting aunt, competent driver and stubborn nurse. Greeley Lassiter played so many roles, she probably didn't know who she was.

He knew who she was. Fern Kelly's daughter.

And idiot that he was, he'd kissed her.

Why didn't he just throw gasoline on a burning car?

He'd come to Aspen because he wanted to use Greeley to open Big Ed's eyes as to Fern's true nature. He'd come because he wanted Greeley to challenge her mother's version about how Greeley ended up in the care of Mary Lassiter.

He hadn't come to kiss Greeley. Or to touch her breast.

He wanted to touch it again. Without clothing.

When had he developed a death wish?

The answer came quickly. When he'd hired Fern Kelly as receptionist because she had a nice, pleasant voice.

Quint closed his eyes and made a derisive sound. Pleasant. There was nothing pleasant about Fern Kelly.

The knock on the door came as a welcome reprieve from his self-recriminations—until Quint answered the door.

A cowboy stood there. The real thing, judging from the

dirt-encrusted boots and the stained hat in his hands. The cowboy's gaze went straight to the cut on Quint's face. "I guess I'm at the right room. You must be Quint Damian."

The cowboy seemed to expect an invitation to come in. Quint stayed in the doorway. "I'm Damian." The cowboy looked familiar, but Quint knew he'd never seen the man before. Allie's husband had darker hair. Under a shock of light brown hair, bright blue eyes regarded Quint steadily. Quint recognized the judgmental stare. "Let me guess," he said with churlish humor, abandoning his post by the door. "You're another one of them, aren't you?"

"If you mean another Lassiter, yes." The cowboy shut the door behind him and extended his hand for a firm shake. "Worth Lassiter. Greeley's brother."

"You have my sympathy."

Lassiter chuckled. "You have sisters?"

"Only child." Quint opened the armoire which held a small bar and refrigerator. "Want a drink?"

"A can of pop if you have one." Lassiter sprawled in an overstuffed chair.

Quint grabbed two soft drinks, then, his hosting duties performed, sat on the sofa. "I suppose you're here to order me out of town."

"I figure you'll leave Aspen when you're ready." Lassiter took a quick swallow.

"Which means you're here to check me out. Want to see my drivers' license and my Social Security card?"

"Cheyenne said you're in your early thirties, heir-apparent to a successful trucking company, industrious, respected, well-liked, single, sought after, but not a playboy."

"I have two fillings in my back molars. How'd she miss those? Does she want to know whether I have high cholesterol and what my blood type is? I expect she already knows how much money I have in the bank."

"Knowing Cheyenne, if she thought those things important, she'd have tracked them down." Lassiter smiled wryly at the expression on Quint's face. "Greeley's her baby sister."

The explanation failed to appease Quint. "I didn't realize Steele ran a detective agency."

"Cheyenne knows people in Denver. Thomas doesn't believe in meddling, so they've arrived at a mutual understanding that she won't burden him when she feels duty-bound to do what's best for someone else."

"I'll bet that sets his mind at ease."

"He'll rope her in if she goes too far," Lassiter said.

"How reassuring."

"The thing is," Lassiter drawled, "as much as the rest of us hate to admit it, Cheyenne's usually on the money. I'd never say it to her face, but she's got a head on her shoulders. While everyone else dithers, she goes right to the heart of a matter."

"Which brings us back to investigating me."

"You didn't think you could wander into our lives, grab up Greeley, and wander out again, did you?"

"Believe it or not," Quint said in a mocking voice, "I did. I thought Greeley would jump at a chance to reunite with her mother."

"No, you didn't. You thought you could persuade or bribe her. What's next? Blackmail?"

"Is that what you've been sent to find out?"

"No." He looked directly at Quint. "I've been sent to cast my vote on whether we help you get what you want."

Quint put down his can. "Get me what I want?"

"Well, help you arrange for Greeley and Fern Kelly to meet. Whether that will result in what you want..." Lassiter shrugged.

"Why?" Quint didn't believe in altruistic fairy godmothers. "The Lassiters have been at great pains to convince me Greeley is more than a half-sister. Why the change of heart?"

"No change of heart. We never think of Greeley as anything other than our sister, but Cheyenne thinks Greeley needs to learn something about herself and who she comes from. The question is, how do we persuade Greeley to confront her demons?''

"And?"

"Cheyenne says you're the answer. According to her research, you're a fair, honest, moral man. Allie thinks you'd never hurt Greeley, on account of what you did for Hannah.''

Quint waved that away. "I happened to be standing there.'' He paused. "You don't say what your mother thinks.''

"Cheyenne learned one other thing about you. When you want something, you go after it. Mom's worried Greeley will be caught in the middle of your battle with Fern. She said when single-minded men go after something, they don't notice who gets hurt.''

The judgment stung, but Quint reminded himself winning a popularity contest wasn't the point. "If you side with your mom, it's two against two.'' Quint didn't need the Lassiters' help to get what he wanted.

Lassiter half-smiled. "It's tied now. Mom has two votes. I'm the swing vote.''

Quint eyed him levelly. "And what do you think?''

Lassiter rolled his can between his palms. "I'm hoping to control any damage.''

Setting down the can, Lassiter stood and extracted a white envelope from his shirt pocket. "Tomorrow night, Cheyenne's having a big society shindig. A combination housewarming, cocktail party and charity benefit at their new house. Invitation only, and going means you have to pledge a hefty sum to Allie's charity for needy and abused animals.'' He handed the envelope to Quint. "An invitation for you and two guests.''

Quint thumbed the edge of the envelope. "Pretty short notice.''

"It's all you're going to get.'' At the door, Lassiter turned. "Be some interesting people there. Jake Norton, the movie actor, and his wife are family friends. They're coming, and there'll be others Fern might like to party with. Some minor royalty. Bigwigs are jetting in from all over the country."

Quint laughed dryly. "Sounds as if you know Fern."

"Her dropping Greeley off when I was ten pretty much defines Fern as far as I'm concerned." He hesitated. "You might want to bear in mind, Cheyenne and Allie won't take kindly to you using and abusing our sister."

"What about you?"

"You don't want to make an enemy of me." The door closed behind Lassiter.

Quint saluted the closed door with his can of pop. Greeley's half-brother knew how to make an exit.

Wandering over to the multipaned window, Quint absently watched large gondolas ferry tourists up and down the mountain rising above the town. Before he came, he hadn't given the Lassiters much thought, but he found he liked them, from Mary on down to Hannah.

He wouldn't have liked Beau Lassiter. Based on the information in the detective's report and from what little Greeley had disclosed, Quint pictured a self-centered rodeo cowboy whose own interests and pleasures always came first.

Quint had never known his father, but he knew exactly what a father should be. Beau Lassiter hadn't been it.

The phone rang, startling him. A beep signaled a fax, and the machine across the room spewed paper. Quint sighed. He needed to check his e-mail and voice mail. He hired capable, qualified people, and taking a few days off now and again had never been a problem, especially now, in the electronic age.

That was all B.F. Before Fern. Big Ed had started the business and, although he was retired, he ought to know better than to listen to Fern's harebrained ideas. Quint blamed Big Ed's overactive sex glands.

He'd call Granddad first, Quint decided. Report in, tell him about the party. How Big Ed got his girlfriend to Aspen was Big Ed's problem.

Quint's problem would be dealing with whatever crisis Fern had precipitated at the trucking terminal.

Belatedly, he realized he should have asked if the Lassiters planned to tell Greeley her mother had been invited to the charity benefit. Big Ed would undoubtedly want to surprise Fern.

Greeley stood in front of her closet trying to decide what to wear. Not that it mattered. Everyone's attention would be riveted on Cheyenne's and Thomas's stunning new home. She had no particular reason for wanting to look her best.

Quint Damian wouldn't be there.

Which had nothing to do with anything. Her breast tingled at the lie. She should have slapped him for touching her. She would have, if he hadn't stopped. Her nipple hardened, and she pulled her robe tighter around her. Her time would be better spent getting dressed instead of standing around mooning over a man who thought he could use sex to manipulate her into doing what he wanted her to do.

What he wanted her to do had nothing to do with sex.

Not that she wanted him to want her to do something with sex.

In fact, she was thrilled he'd finally accepted her refusal to go to Denver. He hadn't called or come to the Double Nickel today.

She certainly had no desire to kiss him again.

A knock sounded at her bedroom door. "You decent?" Worth called.

"Yes. Come on in."

Her mother preceded her brother into the room. The anxious looks on their faces warned Greeley. Her mom and Worth took everything in stride. "Is something wrong?"

"We want to talk to you before we leave for the party." Her mother perched on the edge of Greeley's bed.

"It's nothing you can't handle," Worth said, "but Cheyenne invited Damian to her party."

Greeley turned and looked into her closet, hiding her face before her mother and brother mistakenly thought she welcomed their announcement. She didn't care if Quint came to the party. If she felt light-hearted, well, why not? Parties made everyone happy. "It's Cheyenne's house. She can invite anyone she wants."

She'd wear the gray sheath Cheyenne had bought her in New York City. It was the most elegant dress she owned. Or maybe she should wear her blue-denim jacket and jeans. She wouldn't want him thinking she'd dressed with him in mind. Focused on her internal debate, Greeley didn't immediately register Worth's next words.

"Damian phoned a few minutes ago. His grandfather and Fern Kelly flew into Aspen this afternoon. He's bringing them to Cheyenne's party."

The gray dress fell forgotten to the floor. Quint had kissed her, then betrayed her. Did he really think one little kiss gave him the right to mess with her life?

"Who does he think he is?" She whirled angrily around. "Why didn't you—" The guilty look on her mother's face jolted Greeley. "You knew before he called, didn't you?" A deadening silence confirmed her guess. "Cheyenne's been meddling again, hasn't she?"

Mary Lassiter took a deep breath. "Not just Cheyenne. All of us."

"Why?"

"If you never believe anything else I tell you, Greeley Lassiter, believe this. I love you. I don't care who gave birth to you. As far as I'm concerned, I am your mother. You are as much my child as Worth or Cheyenne or Allie. At some time or other I've wanted to wring all your necks, but I would never, ever allow any of you to stop being my child. Is that clear?"

Greeley gave her mother a direct look. "Since you're my mother, there's no reason for me to meet her."

"You haven't seen her since you were days old, but because she left you, she's always been this festering sore under your skin. It's time you met her and destroyed the hold she has over you, or you'll never truly trust the people who love you."

"I trust you."

"Do you? One time I heard Beau tell you to be good so I wouldn't kick you out," Mary said. "I was so angry, I chewed him out for half an hour. Later I told you to ignore what your father said, that I'd never send you away." Regret filled her eyes. "I don't think you ever quite believed me. Look how often you tested the limits of my love. You never understood there are no limits."

"Quint Damian put this garbage in your head. You never cared before whether I met her. She's not a festering anything. She's nothing."

"I know that," Mary said. "You're the one who doesn't."

"I'm not going. It's all about money to him." Greeley paced across the room. "He thought he could manipulate me by—" Catching Worth's penetrating gaze, Greeley switched gears. "He couldn't persuade me, so he worked on you. You'd think a grown woman would know better than to be influenced by moody green eyes."

Mary sighed and stood. "I've said my piece. You're an adult. Whatever you decide, I'll support." At the bedroom door, she added over her shoulder, "I'll be downstairs waiting for whoever's going." She softly closed the door behind her.

The quiet in the bedroom thickened. "Well?" Greeley finally snapped at her brother. "Go ahead. Get that sermon you're dying to give out of your system."

Worth stretched out on her bed, his hands folded across his middle. "I don't know what it is with my sisters. Always thinking I'm going to point out what they already know."

"She dropped me off like dirty laundry."

"Nah. People return for their laundry."

"Beau never cared one way or the other about me."

"You think that makes you special? He didn't care about any of us."

Greeley walked over to her dresser and played with the belt buckle sitting there. "I was doing all right until he came along."

Worth watched her in the mirror, his thumbs circling each other over his ribcage. "He of the moody green eyes?" he asked in an amused voice. "I sure am curious about how he tried to manipulate you."

"It didn't work. I'm not going to meet her."

Worth hauled his body off the bed. "We'll give you thirty minutes to get your war paint on, then we're leaving."

"I'm not going."

"Up to you, but I thought you had more spine."

They waited forty-five minutes.

Greeley watched the taillights from her mother's car wink around the corner and disappear. They could meet Fern Kelly if they wanted. Greeley had nothing to say to Fern. She didn't want to know what Fern looked like. Didn't care how Fern walked, what she thought.

Didn't give a darn why Fern had abandoned her baby.

There was nothing she wanted to know about Fern.

What if Fern enjoyed using her hands?

No Lassiter, including Worth, enjoyed messing around with the heavy machinery. Except Greeley, who'd learned from Grandpa Yancy.

Yancy was Mary's father. Not Greeley's grandfather.

It would be unbearable if she'd inherited the passions of her life from Fern Kelly. Greeley wanted nothing from Fern.

She looked in the mirror. It was *her* nose. Not Fern's nose. Quint Damian would say anything to connect her to Fern.

She wouldn't be connected.

She wouldn't go.

Not because she was afraid. And not because she had no spine. They could think what they wanted. There was no reason for her to meet Fern Kelly.

There was only Quint Damian's reason. Men like him thought other people existed to accommodate their wishes. He'd been so sure Greeley would jump at the chance to harm Fern Kelly. It would serve him right if she did exactly the opposite.

Greeley picked up the belt buckle that Beau had won at the Greeley Independence Stampede rodeo and absent-mindedly traced the engraved lettering. She could go to the party, listen to Fern's excuses for abandoning her child and pretend to believe every word. She could nod and smile and agree Fern had had no choice. She could act delighted to meet Fern and make insincere promises about their future, knowing Fern had no more desire than Greeley to pursue the relationship. Greeley would never have to see Fern again.

And Quint Damian might think twice the next time he thought about using someone for his own selfish purposes. Did he think a silly little kiss had sucked out her brains to the extent that she'd allow him to create havoc in her life?

She'd show him havoc.

Greeley didn't care what Fern did, where Fern lived, who Fern married.

Quint Damian cared.

Havoc. At Cheyenne's party.

''They must be rolling in dough,'' Fern said in an awed voice, tipping back her head to see to the top of the three-story, stone-trimmed redwood house as Quint helped her from the rented limo. Fern had been jabbering from the second she and his grandfather had stepped out of the plane at the Aspen airport.

Quint wished she'd shut up. His head ached. The overwhelming scent of the perfume she'd applied with a heavy hand roiled his stomach.

A man, probably security, stood solidly at the door checking invitations. Quint almost wished for a problem with theirs, denying them entry.

Now that it was too late, he knew the whole idea stunk. Lack of oxygen at this high altitude must have killed half his brain cells. The meeting was going to be a disaster, and Granddad would blame him. Quint winced at the thought of Fern's and Greeley's reactions.

Even if she was Fern's daughter, he shouldn't have let himself be talked into this.

His lips tightened in self-disgust as he rejected the shifting of responsibility. Nobody had talked him into anything. He'd embraced the plan. Convinced himself her adoptive family knew best.

Why was he beating himself up over this? A woman's family did know best. Greeley had been making a big deal out of a simple little meeting. Fern had given birth to Greeley. So what? Once they'd exchanged a few polite words, Greeley would see the puny biological connection meant nothing. There was no reason for her to get upset.

There was no reason for him to regret setting up the meeting. He'd done nothing that shouldn't have been done years ago. Greeley would thank him once the ordeal was over.

Fern was going into raptures over the pink marble floor in the two-story-high entryway when Quint spotted Greeley.

She stood with her back to him. Blue jeans hugged the curves of her hips. His mouth went dry. He'd never particularly noticed a woman's bottom before. He wanted to caress hers.

He forced himself to dispassionately study her. Her size came from her mother, although Fern's body was slightly rounder than her daughter's. Greeley's brown hair hung straight down her back, while Fern's skillfully cut hair had been colored an expensive shade of platinum. Quint had seen the bill.

"Quint. Welcome." Cheyenne Steele curved her left arm

around his. "This must be your grandfather." She extended her right hand. "I'm glad you could come. I'm Cheyenne Steele."

The name meant nothing to Fern, who gushed with flattery. Quint saw Cheyenne's subtle signal, and Steele appeared with Jake Norton and his wife. Quint muttered all the right words as his gaze scanned the huge room looking for Lassiters.

They weren't hard to find. Maybe it was the anxiety each seemed to give off. Maybe it was the way each focused uneasily on Greeley. Maybe it was the way Mary Lassiter looked ten years older than she had yesterday.

The Lassiters had had second thoughts. Quint silently cursed. This was going to be a flaming car wreck.

Greeley turned around, and Quint immediately understood the cause of the Lassiters' misgivings. Greeley knew.

Fire-engine-red lipstick and heavily made-up eyes formed a garish triangle of color in an otherwise colorless face. Under her faded blue-denim jacket, silver metallic fabric molded her upper body. Quint had seen women in more revealing outfits, but for some reason those women hadn't looked half as indecent as Greeley did. Every man at the party must be thinking about her breasts. And picturing her naked in his bed. Excusing himself with the barest minimum of politeness, Quint strode across the floor.

She saw him coming. The bitter, scorching anger in her eyes almost stopped him. Almost. He kept going.

"How'd you find out?" he asked.

"Mom and Worth told me."

"They allowed you to come to the party half-nude?" He wanted to rip off his jacket and cover her up.

"We came in separate cars."

The huge expanse of bare skin exposed by her plunging neckline was filled with the most incredible piece of jewelry Quint had ever seen. Unable to believe his eyes, he peered closer. "Those are car parts."

"Give the man a prize for being so smart." Her white face and the way the necklace trembled belied her cool voice.

Quint captured the necklace in one hand. The metal retained the warmth of her skin. The back of his knuckles grazed her chest, and he forgot everything but how much he wanted her. A key soldered to the assembled parts caught his eye. He rubbed it with his thumb. "The key to your heart?"

"It's an old car key. My heart's not so easily accessed."

Blue-gray eyes had always seemed dull to him before. The misconception amused him. This woman would never be dull. "I think it's more than that."

"Suit yourself. You always do."

A little color had returned to her face. Quint retained hold of the necklace. "You didn't ask about my injury," he said in an aggrieved voice.

"Since you spent the day plotting with my family behind my back, you're obviously fine."

"Thanks for calling to check on me this morning."

"I didn't call. Who told you I did? I didn't leave my name."

He gave her a slow smile. "The telephone operator recognized your voice."

"I would have checked on anyone who'd been injured while saving Hannah from disaster."

Quint raised an eyebrow. "And kissed them better."

"And kissed them better," she said defiantly.

He stared at her lips. "I feel a relapse coming on."

Red flagged her cheekbones. "Fight it."

He shook his head. "I don't want to. I want to kiss you." He raised his gaze to capture hers. "I wonder what you'd do if I kissed you right here, right now." She'd bewitched him. He didn't care where they were, who she was, who was watching. He wanted to kiss her. He wanted to push away the scraps of silver material and play with her breasts. He wanted to peel off her jeans and curve his hands over her bottom. He wanted to know if her skin was as warm and silky and alive as it looked. He wanted to make love to her on the marble floor.

He wanted to make love to Fern Kelly's daughter.

Her eyes told him a million and one things. He ignored them all. Except one. The one that said she might not object if he kissed her.

He could always think later about who she was.

"Going to introduce us to your friend?" his grandfather's hearty voice came from behind Quint.

"Yes," Quint said. Panic flashed through Greeley's eyes, and he knew he couldn't force her to meet her mother in front of a crowd of people. Metal and hard plastic bit into his palm, and he released her necklace, taking her cold hand instead. Where could they find privacy?

Greeley didn't seem to notice he held her hand.

Someone tugged his trousers. "Hi, Mr. Damian, I've been waiting for you!" Hannah beamed up at him. "This is my cousin, Davy. He's my very best friend."

The young boy gave Quint a wide grin. "Mom said you have lots of big trucks. I'm Davy Steele."

"Silly, I already told him your name." Hannah held out her hand to Quint. "I want to show you something outdoors."

Fern and Greeley could meet there, away from prying eyes. Quint gave the child his free hand. "Let's all go outside and see what Hannah wants to show me."

Greeley stiffened in resistance for a fraction of a second before allowing Quint to tug her toward the French doors.

Hannah wanted to show him another statue. "Can you see all the hearts? It's Davy's and his mama's and daddy's. It's called Kinds of Love, 'cause his other mama and daddy loved him but they're playing with angels so Aunt Cheyenne and Uncle Thomas are his new mama and daddy and they love him now." She appeared ready to expand on the subject, but Thomas came and whisked the children back into the house.

Quint didn't exactly relax, but Hannah's removal from the

scene averted the possibility of the little girl calling her aunt by name. Uncharacteristically indecisive, Quint hesitated. Belatedly, he realized he should have brought the two women together in Denver where he could control the fallout.

Greeley took the matter into her own hands. Pulling free of his grasp, she turned to the older couple. "You must be Quint's grandfather, and you're Fern Kelly."

Fern barely acknowledged her name. "Their house shows such exquisite taste. Why do you suppose they have a monstrosity like this in their courtyard?"

"I made it for them for a wedding present," Greeley said.

Fern rushed into speech. "I'm sure it's a very valuable piece. I'm not much of an art person. Are you an artist I should know of? I didn't catch your name."

The light streaming through the French doors to the house revealed the faint, fixed smile on Greeley's lips. "That's because Quint hustled us outdoors before he told you who I am. In case one of us caused a scene."

Fern shot Quint a significant look from under lowered lashes. "I can't imagine why he would think something so silly."

Fern thought he was trying to make her jealous. Quint had a very bad feeling. This could be worse than he feared.

"Because I'm Greeley Lassiter. You gave birth to me twenty-four years ago."

Fern tottered backward on her high heels. "You're her?"

"Surprise!" Big Ed boomed. "I wanted to get my best girl something special for a wedding present, and I asked myself, what better present than to give her back her little girl?" He beamed at Greeley. "You're just as pretty as your mother."

The two women stared at each other for what seemed an eternity, then Fern made a choking sound and ran back into the house.

Big Ed turned an embarrassed smile on Greeley. "Having you sprung on her like this probably overexcited her. But don't you worry, Ms. Lassiter, you two can do your catching up later. I know Fern is thrilled to see you again.'' He followed Fern into the house.

"Satisfied?" Greeley asked.

CHAPTER FOUR

FERN'S BEHAVIOR might have raised some doubt in Big Ed's mind, but Quint felt little satisfaction. Greeley's toneless voice made him uneasy. He snorted in silent derision at the bland word. *Uneasy* didn't come close to describing the way his entire insides had knotted up. Light glinted off her abnormally large, deep-set eyes. Dark, bottomless holes in a deathly pale face.

He'd feel better if she socked him in the jaw.

From the beginning she'd said she didn't want to see her mother. Intent on his goal, he'd ignored her wishes, hadn't tried to see the situation from her viewpoint. He'd sacrificed her feelings to save his grandfather and his grandfather's business from Fern.

His conscience jabbed him. Okay, maybe he'd been thinking of himself, too.

Heroes saved women and children. They didn't sacrifice them.

He'd never be a hero.

She shouldn't have expected him to act like a hero. Her stricken behavior was an act to make him feel guilty. Worth and Mary had told her before she came that her mother would be at the party. "Nobody put a gun to your head and forced you to come."

"I know," she said listlessly.

"What did you think she was going to do? Throw her arms around you and weep tears of joy over being reunited with you? Don't tell me you believed someone forced her to get rid of you," he ground out, frustrated by an inability to dispel her apathy. "You know very well she didn't want you, so she dumped you."

Greeley's eyes filled her face as she stared at him, then she turned and walked rapidly away from the house.

Taken by surprise, it took Quint a minute to catch up with her. He reached for her arm and pulled her to a stop. "Where are you going?"

"What do you care?"

He tightened his grip as she tried to break free. "Look, I'm sorry. Maybe springing you on Fern wasn't the world's best idea, but nothing's changed in your life."

"You don't know anything. Let go of me."

Feeling her bones trembling beneath his touch, Quint sensed she was a hairbreadth away from falling to pieces. "Sit on that bench, and I'll go after Mary."

"This has nothing to do with my family." She twisted in his grasp. "Let go of me."

"What's going on here?" A burly man stood in their path.

"She's not feeling well, so we're leaving," Quint said.

"You have to go out the way you came. This gate is locked."

For the first time Quint noticed the stone wall enclosing the large courtyard. "You must have the key."

"Maybe, but you still have to leave through the front door."

"This is Mrs. Steele's half-sister."

"I'll get Mrs. Steele." The security man pulled out a small two-way radio.

"No," Greeley said. "I just want to leave. Quietly."

"Ask for Mr. Steele," Quint said. "You can describe her. He won't have to come out."

The man muttered into the radio. Then, listening, he studied Greeley, nodding his head. "What's the name of your niece's paint horse?"

"Honey," Greeley said.

"Yeah, okay," he said into the radio, then pocketed it. "Okay, folks. Sorry about that. Can't be too careful. They own a bunch of expensive art, and the ladies are wearing some pretty pricey jewelry." He unlocked the gate.

"No problem," Quint said. "Thanks."

Outside the courtyard, transportation became his next problem. The limo wasn't due back for hours.

"Hi, Greeley. Leaving already?" A young man materialized from the dark. "I'll get your truck." The parking attendant disappeared.

A few minutes later headlights swept around the house. The attendant stepped out of a beat-up pickup, leaving the motor running. Quint guided Greeley into the passenger side. Her meek compliance disturbed him more than anything thus far. Quint handed the man a bill. "Tell Steele, Greeley left with Quint Damian and ask him to tell my grandfather."

Quint said nothing had changed. Nothing had.

Everything had.

Growing up and facing reality stunk.

The silly little fantasy Greeley had hoarded deep in the recesses of her heart from about age five had been shattered in the space of one hysterical cry.

Her mother had told her why Fern brought Greeley to Mary. A single mother of limited means, Fern didn't have the resources to care for a baby.

For all intents and purposes, Mary Lassiter had been a single mom. With three children of her own.

Greeley's mom put a positive spin on how a birth mother could abandon her child. She claimed Fern had loved her baby very much and proof of that love was the way she'd wanted a good life for her daughter. As Greeley grew older, Mary said Fern kept away because she didn't want her child forced to choose between two mothers.

Choosing would have been easy. Mary Lassiter would always be Greeley's mother.

Leaning against the seat back, Greeley stared into the black night, unable to erase from her mind the look on Fern Kelly's face. Women who carried you in their wombs for nine months, who gave birth to you, weren't supposed to take one look at you and recoil in horror. Most didn't.

What was wrong with Greeley that the woman who'd brought her into this world had been unable to love her?

Quint Damian's muttering broke through her torturous thoughts. She glanced in his direction. He spoke quietly into her cellular phone. Checking on the success of his little scheme? Assuring her family he wouldn't let her slit her wrists?

Or calling his girlfriend. Did he love his girlfriend or only want sex? Maybe with men it was always sex. It had been with Beau.

Quint hung up the phone.

"Do you have sex a lot?"

Quint almost ran the pickup off the road. Bringing the truck under control, he asked explosively, "What kind of question is that?"

"Beau had sex wherever he happened to be. You know how they say sailors have a girl in every port? Beau had one in every rodeo town. After Mom gave birth to Worth, she stayed on the ranch while Beau rodeoed. Every time he got injured, he'd run home to Mom and she'd nurse him back to health. To thank her, he'd leave her pregnant. He met Fern in Greeley. Isn't that rich? I'm named after the town where my father fornicated with a woman."

The matter-of-fact recitation chilled him. As if she were reciting ingredients in a recipe rather than discussing her father's moral failings.

"Two self-centered, sex-crazy people having a good time and dumping the consequences on someone else." Greeley rocked back and forth, her forward motion limited by her shoulder safety strap. "I'm not a love child. I'm a lust child."

"Your stepmother loves you."

"Stepmother. Half-sisters. Half-brother. Do you know what it's like, going through life as a half-person? Of course

you don't. Sure, they love me. Pity and compassion run
through my family, from Mom on down. They take in all
kinds of strays, from three-legged cats and rescued grey-
hounds to kids in need of a parent or two. Cheyenne felt
sorry for Davy. Allie felt sorry for Hannah, and Mom felt
sorry for me. People felt sorry for Mom because I got
dumped on her, or sorry for me because the woman who gave
birth to me couldn't love me. Don't you feel sorry for me?"

"No," he lied. "You feel sorry enough for both of us."

"Add self-pity to my sins. I have a lot. Beau used to warn
me I'd better behave or Mom would regret taking me in."

"I wouldn't have liked your father." The man should have
been tarred and feathered and run out of town on a rail.

"Beau was raised in foster homes. He got kicked out a
lot."

"That's no reason for him—"

She cut him off. "I should have a curl in the middle of
my forehead. I used to act either very good so Mom wouldn't
kick me out, or I'd be very bad, testing her, seeing how far
I could go before she kicked me out."

"I've just met Mary, but I know she's not the type to do
that."

"No, she's a good person, one of the best. Mom said
Fern's always been a festering sore with me, but she wasn't.
Not really. I used to try and picture what she'd look like. I
knew she'd be beautiful. Like a princess or a fairy god-
mother. When I was little I'd tell kids at school she'd had to
go away. I invented hundreds of reasons why. Amnesia or
wrongful imprisonment. A missionary on the other side of
the world. Nobody ever believed me."

"Except maybe you?"

She shrugged. "Maybe, when I was very young. Later, I
knew she'd never magically appear to explain how she'd
been forced to abandon me. I knew she wasn't ever going to
tell me she loved me and the reason she'd gotten rid of me

wasn't because I was an ugly baby or cried too much or anything.''

Quint had a sinking feeling that up until the moment Fern ran from her daughter, Greeley had secretly clung to her childish fantasies. In forcing her to face her mother, he'd stolen Greeley's dreams. ''Her abandoning you had nothing to do with you,'' he said harshly. ''Fern puts her wants before anything else. I can almost guarantee you she planned to dump her baby from the second she discovered she was pregnant.''

''And that's my heritage. Aren't I proud?''

''Forget it.''

''How does one forget where the blood in her veins came from? Worth used to fret he'd grow up as irresponsible as Beau. Grandpa—Yancy Nichols, Mom's dad—said Worth shouldn't worry, he was Mom's kid, too, and the good from Mom would muscle out the bad from Beau. But I don't have any of Mom in me.''

Quint didn't like the direction of her conversation. ''Environment's more important than heredity when it comes to stuff like that. People aren't born good or bad. Mary raised you. That's what counts.''

She shook her head. ''I was raised on a ranch. I know what goes into the computer. A cow's breeding, not where she was raised. Bloodlines count. There's no Nichols blood in me. Just Fern's and Beau's. Beau could smile charmingly and ride anything with four legs. Name some of Fern's positive qualities.''

He racked his brain to come up with something. *Anything*.

Greeley gave a mirthless laugh. ''That's what I thought. Let's see. Fern is careless, selfish, irresponsible. Not to mention a thief. I say that because sleeping with another woman's husband is a kind of theft. I've never stolen anything, but I'm young. Give me time.''

''You're going a little overboard here, aren't you?''

She tipped her head, as if giving serious consideration to

his rhetorical question. "No, I don't think so. I look at Fern and see my future. You think she's a gold-digger. What else is she?"

"Why do you ask? Are you planning to emulate her?"

"Why not?" she asked in a flippant voice.

"I can give you a million reasons," he said, annoyed with her single-minded insistence on being stupidly illogical. He sensed her appraising him. "What?"

"You didn't answer my question earlier. Do you have sex a lot?"

"That's none of your business." Quint gripped the steering wheel so tightly, it was a wonder it didn't snap in half. She'd make him as crazy as she was.

"You don't have to go sanctimonious on me. I'm tired of waiting for my bad genes to kick in, so I've decided to give them a jump start."

The air between them practically quivered. He suspected he didn't want to know the answer, but he couldn't help asking the question. "What does that have to do with my sex life?"

"You're the other half of history repeating itself. Stranger rides into town. Like mother, like daughter. No tender feelings. Just you and me and naked bodies and lust. Fueled by my bad blood, of course."

"That is the most idiotic thing I've ever heard. What makes you think I'd be interested in sleeping with you?" His body was definitely interested. He reminded himself who she was. He had no intention of sleeping with Fern's daughter.

"Men are always interested in sex."

"Spoken through your vast experience, no doubt," he said in a belittling voice.

"Are you saying you're not interested in sex?"

"Sex? Or some kind of bizarre payback because Fern didn't go all gooey and dream of baby powder once she saw you?"

"I hate you."

"That settles the sex thing then, doesn't it?" He ignored a sharp pang of regret. If he slept with her, he'd really regret it. Afterward.

"I don't have to like you to have sex with you. We'd just take off our clothes and get into bed together."

"Quit acting so childish or I'll—"

"What? Spank me? Do you think Fern is into kinky sex?"

Quint tamped down his rising fury. And rising lust. "I don't want to spank you," he said through his teeth. Strip her naked, yes, but spanking wasn't what he had in mind. "I'd like to shake some sense into you."

"You can't. I'm sure Fern has no sense. If she did, she never would have taken up with Beau, much less been stupid enough to get pregnant."

They drove in silence for about five minutes. Quint didn't even want to think about what crazy ideas were going through her brain now. Instead he found himself thinking about the shiny silver cloth covering her breasts. And visualized himself slowly removing it. Along with every other stitch of clothing she wore. His imagination conjured up a picture of her bare bottom.

"It's beautiful, but you won't be able to see much."

"What?" Could she read his mind?

"Independence Pass. That's where you're headed, isn't it? It's one of the most beautiful views in Colorado."

Quint had been driving aimlessly, with no destination in mind. He didn't know where to take her, but he had no intention of leaving her alone. In her current weird frame of mind, there was no predicting what she'd do. Ahead of them, the highway tunneled through trees. Spotting a side road leading to a campground, Quint pulled off the highway and parked.

"Having sex in the cab of my pickup suits me, but maybe we ought to find a more secluded place. We might get arrested." She paused. "Of course, Fern's daughter being arrested probably wouldn't surprise anyone. Blood always tells."

He turned sideways in his seat. "Do you think you'll finish throwing your infantile temper tantrum any time soon?"

A passing car briefly illuminated the truck's interior. Greeley looked straight ahead, clutching her shoulder strap as if it were the only thing keeping her from flying into a million pieces. Her silver top had twisted, and for a breath-taking second, a breast gleamed white in the headlights.

"I asked you to have sex with me," she said. "Don't you want to?"

He wanted to. Badly.

He had no intention of giving in to his desires.

Or of being manipulated by the little catch in her voice.

Greeley Lassiter didn't want to be held or wanted or loved. She wasn't miserable and she wasn't sexually aroused.

She was furious at her mother's treatment and wanted to hit back at Fern any way she could. As if it mattered to Fern whether Greeley slept with the entire male population of Colorado.

The smartest move Quint could make was to return to Cheyenne's house and turn Greeley over to her stepmother. Let Mary deal with her stepdaughter. Quint hadn't been the only one involved in setting up this fiasco.

Who knew she'd turn into a nutcase?

He removed his seat belt and slid toward her. Slipping his hand beneath Greeley's top, he eased the fabric back in place. Her skin scorched his fingers. Impossible not to indulge himself by toying, if only for a second, with the hardened tip. Her red lips looked black in the dark, but no less inviting.

Quint succumbed to temptation. He deserved a kiss for showing gentlemanly, if not superhuman, restraint.

Her mouth trembled under his. Cradling her face, he used his thumb to gently pull her lips apart. She stiffened, then rammed her tongue into his mouth. It took all Quint's will-power to pull back, his lips caressing her tongue as he disengaged.

"Hotel," he said. A man could have too many scruples. He cleared the hoarseness from his voice. "We'll be more comfortable there."

She shrugged. "Hotel bed, pickup, on the ground...makes no difference to me. Rumor is I was conceived on the floor behind the bar in a salon."

Quint fastened his seat belt with a snap. Her death grip on her shoulder strap the entire length of his kiss hadn't escaped his notice. Wondering how long it would take before she changed her mind, he turned and drove rapidly to the hotel.

Palpable waves of tension flowed from her, but she said nothing. He concentrated on the curving highway. If he thought about her in his bed, they'd never make it to Aspen.

Turning her truck over to the bellman, Quint followed Greeley through the massive double doors into the three-story lobby. Her boot heels clicked against the marble tiles. In the wood-paneled elevator car, Greeley stared straight ahead, her dark hair a curtain shielding her thoughts. He brushed aside her hair and she jerked around to face him. The startled movement sent waves of flowery scent into the air.

And reinforced the panic in her eyes. A panic at war with her determined chin.

Remorse belted him in the stomach. Remorse and regret. He didn't take advantage of hurting, vulnerable women, and he didn't sleep with frightened little girls who'd started something they didn't want to finish. His jaw tightened. He wanted her—badly, but Damians did the honorable thing.

Her eyes told him it would be wrong to have sex with her.

Her chin told him getting out of it wouldn't be easy.

He couldn't pat her on the head and send her home. No matter what he said, no matter how he explained his decision, she'd feel rejected. Unwanted.

Again.

He sensed she teetered dangerously near an emotional

chasm. Another rejection might send her screaming over the edge. He couldn't risk it. She had to reject him.

All he had to do was give her a reason.

The elevator zoomed upward at the speed of light. Quint Damian played with her hair and looked at her as if he were a chocoholic and she a giant box of chocolate candy, his for the unwrapping.

She couldn't go through with it.

How could she have told him she wanted to have sex with him? She couldn't have sex with a stranger.

The elevator stopped and he smiled at her, practically drooling.

She wanted to go home. Cold air in the hallway swirled about her, plunging down her bare neckline. She should have worn the gray dress.

At his suite, he unlocked the door and stood back to let her enter. She smiled weakly and walked into the lion's den.

"We'll definitely require this." He held up the Do Not Disturb sign before hanging it on the outside doorknob. All he needed above his sinister grin was a long mustache to tweak. He locked the door. Double-locked it and bolted it.

Not to keep people out; to keep her in.

Draping a heavy arm over her shoulder, he practically dragged her into the sitting room. "This is cozy, isn't it?"

She agreed, for lack of anything better to say. The day he'd lain injured on the sofa, the room had seemed light and airy. She hadn't paid much attention to the ceiling border of entwined green vines sinuously curving around the room or the lush, elegantly erotic flowers flowing across the pale green carpet. A dark green velvet sofa beckoned with voluptuous curves and soft pillows.

Fleeing from the sofa and all it suggested, Greeley practically raced across the room to stand in front of a large framed print hanging on the opposite wall. She stared blindly at the picture as she desperately sought a way out of this nightmarish situation she'd put herself into.

"An olden days pin-up girl," Quint said.

Greeley blinked and looked at the print. And berated her lousy lack of judgment in choosing to stand there. A scantily clad maiden curved provocatively around a large urn, sipping from a crystal goblet, a come-hither look in her eyes. "She must be advertising wine," Greeley managed to say. Hotels should hang prints of mountain scenery.

"Sex sold products then, still does. Speaking of liquid refreshment, I'll fix us drinks while you take off your clothes, babe."

"I thought we could talk first," Greeley said quickly.

"We can talk later. What we want has nothing to do with getting to know each other. We want sex. I like that in a woman. A man gets tired of all that foreplay junk. The trouble with you women is you read too many magazines, and you get weird ideas in your head. Wham, bam, thank you, ma'am, that's what women need, right, babe?"

"Actually, I think I need a little more than—"

"Yeah, I heard you out there in the car." He leered at her. "I knew you were my kind of woman when you starting talking about playing games."

"Games?" She didn't think he meant card games.

"Spanking. I haven't tried that one, but if that's what turns you on, babe, I'm game. We've got all night." His heavy-lidded gaze slowly caressed her body. "Why do you think I put out that sign? I'm looking forward to a night of marathon sex. I like a woman who doesn't insist on conditions or flowers or promises or commitment before she puts out. Just get naked and have sex. You and I are going to get along great, babe, just great."

"I need to use the ladies' room," Greeley said in a panic.

"Sure." He leered at her again. "Don't be long, now."

Locking the bathroom door, she sank to the edge of the marble bathtub. Now what? He'd turned into a monster.

Which was entirely her fault. She'd given him every reason to think his behavior would be acceptable to her. She'd suggested having sex; he hadn't. No wonder he was licking his chops.

She had to get away.

Would he believe "no" at this late date?

A fist pounded on the door. "Hey, babe, you okay in there?"

"Yes, I'll be out in a minute." Her voice came out high and squeaky. She sounded like a ten-year-old. A phone by the shower caught her eye. She could call the front desk. Tell them...tell them what? That she'd told Quint Damian she wanted to have sex, and now she'd changed her mind, but didn't know how to tell him, so would they please come upstairs and rescue her from this embarrassing predicament?

And do it without gossiping about it all over town? She could hear the comments. "What did you expect? She's illegitimate, you know. Her biological mother slept around and then dumped her off on Mary Lassiter. Always knew she'd grow up to be like her mother. Poor Mary. She tried so hard."

Her mother, her real mother, Mary, would hear the gossip and be humiliated and hurt.

No, Greeley could not call the front desk.

"Getting impatient out here, babe. You falling asleep in there or something?"

"I'm almost done." She stood and turned the faucet on full force. A clown's face stared at her from the bathroom mirror.

Worth was only a phone call away, but that might be too far. If he arrived too late, he'd feel compelled to slug Quint Damian. News of the ensuing brawl would be all over town by morning. Hurting Worth and their mother.

She was a little old to expect her big brother to rescue her from the mess she'd created.

Think, Greeley, think!

The bathroom came equipped with every luxury. Except one. No window. Even if there was one, the suite was on the third floor.

Quint Damian banged impatiently on the door again. "Taking you long enough." His voice took on an oily tinge. "Planning some kind of surprise for me, babe?"

"Uh, yes. I'm almost ready." Ready for what?

Suddenly the bathroom door shuddered under the impact of a fist, and muttered swear words came from the other side.

Greeley's heart stopped. She'd run out of time. "What?"

"When you said 'ready,' it reminded me. I'm not. I mean, events kind of took me by surprise, babe. I wasn't expecting to jump in the sack with you tonight. I need to go out for a minute."

"Go out?"

"Get some protection. I saw a drugstore down the street. Help yourself to something in the bar. Knowing you'll be spread out stark naked on the sofa will get me back here in record time. Now don't go away, babe. I'll be right back."

Greeley gave him a three-minute head start, then she dashed from the suite and down the back stairs. Convincing the bellman to let her go with him to her car in the parking garage took less than a second and a decent tip.

She didn't bother to leave a note for Quint Damian. How would she have signed it? Babe?

Quint hid in the hallway around the corner until he heard Greeley's footsteps take off in the opposite direction. He ought to win an Academy Award for his performance. As he watched her streak through the doorway to the staircase, he hoped she was headed home.

He'd done the honorable thing. Sent her on her way. Greeley Lassiter was no longer his responsibility. Let the Lassiters worry about her now. He could wipe her out of his mind. And his life.

No, he couldn't. Not at this time of night. Heaving a resigned sigh, Quint took the elevator to the lobby. Greeley drove past the front of the hotel while he waited for his car to be brought around.

He had no problem catching up with her. She turned onto the highway and headed north toward Hope Valley and her stepmother's ranch. He could return to the hotel.

Hanging back so she wouldn't recognize his car in her rearview mirror, he kept pace with her.

The light traffic allowed him to use his cell phone, and he dialed the Lassiter house. No one answered. After a moment's thought, he dialed the hotel desk and requested that someone contact Steele and ask him to have Worth Lassiter phone Quint Damian. He gave the hotel operator his cell phone number.

Lassiter rang back minutes later.

"I think she's on her way home," Quint said without preamble. "She doesn't know I'm following her. I don't know what she'll do once she gets there."

"Got it. Mom and I are on the way."

Greeley Lassiter knew how to drive. Too fast, but definitely under control. He suspected she made an art out of control. She certainly tried to control her emotions. Probably believed she did. Her eyes betrayed her.

The pickup's brake lights came on, and then its headlights swept up the road leading between the canyon walls. Quint dropped farther back. Several cars came from the other direction, and he'd noticed a car a distance ahead of her before the hills blocked it from view. She'd never notice him following her.

When Greeley turned in at the ranch, he kept going, not doubling back until he'd driven over a small hill out of sight. Back at the gate, he extinguished his headlights and parked well off the road. It was less than a quarter of a mile from the gate to the house. He hoped the dog wouldn't bark.

Lights came on inside the house. Quint leaned against the trunk of the large cottonwood and waited. Almost at once the front door opened. The black Lab limped out and looked directly at Quint. Quint froze, then remembered the dog was practically blind. The dog moved stiffly off the porch and headed in Quint's direction. He greeted Quint with a nudge and a low woof.

"You're a big help," Quint muttered and reached down to scratch behind the dog's ears. "Do your business and get back in the house before she comes looking for you."

The Lab enthusiastically wagged his tail.

Quint saw Greeley's silhouette at the door and quickly ducked behind the tree. Greeley called the dog.

Shadow followed him around the tree.

Greeley's footsteps sounded on the porch. She called again.

The dog barked. Probably inviting her to join the party, Quint thought morosely. All he needed was for Greeley to find him here. He'd never be able to explain.

"Shadow? Where are you?" She came down the steps and started across the yard, her feet crunching gravel. The dog barked as lights swept into the ranch yard. The Lassiters had arrived home.

The driver shut off the engine, doors slammed and Mary greeted Greeley. Quint couldn't distinguish their words as they moved toward the house. Then Greeley stopped and called to her half-brother about the dog.

"He's probably treed a big, bad rustler," Lassiter said in a low voice as he neared the cottonwood.

"This dog wouldn't tree a rustler if the guy was chasing off your entire herd."

Lassiter laughed. "Is this how you always escort women home?"

"It's how I escort crazy people home," Quint retorted.

After a moment, Lassiter asked, "That bad? Were you worried she'd harm herself?"

Lassiter's question gave form to Quint's amorphous fears. "I didn't know if she'd do anything, well, foolish."

"Foolish, yes. My sisters thrive on doing foolish things. But not suicidal."

"I didn't say—"

"But you thought it. Why?"

Quint gave Worth an edited version of Fern's reaction and Greeley's response.

"You left the party quite a while ago."

Quint knew a question when he heard one, no matter how it was worded. "We drove around awhile, before going back to the hotel for a drink. Greeley decided she didn't want a drink, and she came home. I followed her home to make sure she made it okay."

"I don't suppose you're going to tell me what happened in your hotel room."

"I didn't say we went to my room."

"Get real, Damian, my brother-in-law owns the hotel. I know exactly what time you two returned there."

"The next time I'm in Aspen I'll stay at the Hotel Jerome," Quint said coolly. "As it happens, however, nothing happened in my room."

If Greeley wanted to tell her half-brother she'd invited herself into Quint's bed before having second thoughts, that was her business.

Quint had other business to attend to. Starting with a cold shower.

CHAPTER FIVE

"WHY ARE YOU standing in the dark?"

Greeley didn't turn at her mother's question. "Don't switch on the light."

"I'm sorry your meeting with Fern didn't go well, but brooding won't change anything."

"Uh-huh."

"The one I feel sorry for is Fern. After missing the first twenty-four years of your life, she's blown a chance to get to know you. That's really sad. She's missing a lot."

"Uh-huh."

"Greeley Lassiter, are you listening to me? What is so interesting out that window?"

"Worth talking to Quint Damian."

"What would Quint be doing here this time of night?"

"He followed me home. Somebody ought to tell him if he's going to spy on people, he needs to drive a car with a less distinctive silhouette."

Her mother joined her at the window. "All I see is Worth talking to Shadow."

"Quint's hiding behind the tree."

"Really, Greeley, I know you've had an upsetting evening, but I think your imagination has run amuck."

"Oh, Mom, you know he's there. When you drove in, you must have seen his car up by the gate. He's been skulking around, so I sicced Shadow on him."

Her mother came close to giggling.

Greeley laughed with her. "I know. Shadow apparently recognized the scent of his new best friend and made a bee-line for him. Next time I'll get out Grandpa's old shotgun."

After a second, she asked casually, "Whose idea was it that he follow me? His or yours?"

"I don't know why—"

"I called Cheyenne's place to tell you I was home. The caterer answered the phone and said Worth received a message, made a phone call and you left immediately. I can add two and two. Were you that worried?" She felt her mother shrug in the dark.

"More guilt than worry. Instead of respecting your wishes, we pushed you into doing something you didn't want to do, and it went badly. Since you four became adults, I've tried to keep from interfering in your lives. I don't know why I didn't mind my own business this time. Fear and jealousy, I guess."

Greeley looked at her mother in surprise. "About what?"

"That you'd prefer her. That, after all these years, you'd decide she made a better mother and you'd wish she'd raised you."

"That's the most ridiculous thing I've ever heard. You're the best mother in the world, and I'll always be grateful to you for taking me in."

"I fell in love with Worth and Cheyenne and Allie the second I saw their little wrinkled faces for the first time. The only difference with you is you were a few days older the first time I saw you. I tried to be the best mother to all four of you that I could be." Mary hesitated. "I don't need or want gratitude from any of you."

Greeley put her arm around her mother's waist and laid her head on her shoulder. When she could speak, she said in a deliberately teasing voice, "We all know what you want from us. Grandchildren."

Her mother gave her a quick squeeze. "You bet. Any prospects?"

"What are you two doing in the dark?" Worth asked from the hallway.

"Watching you two junior spies stumble around outside," Greeley said.

Worth laughed. "Don't tell Damian that. He's convinced he's the sneakiest person in the state of Colorado."

"I'm sure he's that," Greeley said flatly.

She'd figured it out within minutes of spotting his car in her rearview mirror. Her first impulse had been to drive straight to the police station and charge him with stalking. Fortunately, clearer thinking took over and Greeley realized she'd been an unsuspecting participant in a total farce.

The entire evening had been a farce. Everyone had played a part, and sorting out the various players and their motives kept Greeley awake most of the night.

Worth and her sisters had been meddling but sincere. One of the chief hazards of being the youngest child. Everyone knew better than you exactly what you should do.

Her mother's fears had served as an eye-opener. Greeley and her mom loving each other, yet doubting the other's love. Merely because they hadn't shared an umbilical cord.

They'd fallen prey to a sentiment they condemned in others. Assuming biological bonds were stronger than bonds forged through love. Quiet moments, shared secrets, working together, homework help, advice—these and more defined the relationship between a mother and child.

For years Greeley had claimed she was not Fern Kelly's daughter. This morning she believed it.

There remained one cloud on her horizon. One very large, very dark cloud. Quint Damian.

Greeley viciously hammered a bumper, reshaping it to form part of the massive hindquarters of an arrogant, strutting bull elk. She didn't care if she never saw Quint Damian again. She hoped she never saw him again. She *refused* to see him again.

Recalling her behavior last night made her face burn. Besides spouting all kinds of nonsense about her bad blood, she'd practically demanded he have sex with her.

Last night had been the low point—or high comedic point, depending on one's perspective—of her young life. Two highly dramatic, unique rejections. If she hadn't allowed Fern's behavior to deaden her brain, Greeley would have seen Quint's exaggerated portrayal of an oversexed male for what it was. The desperate act of a man who wanted to get her, not out of her clothes, but out of his suite.

The ridiculous charade insulted her. Did he really think she was so pathetic he couldn't simply tell her he wasn't interested? He didn't have to treat her as if she were ten years old or on the brink of a nervous breakdown. She would have appreciated it if he'd treated her as an adult.

It wasn't her fault he'd panicked. A person would think she'd knocked him to the floor and tried to rip off his clothes. Did he act like an idiot every time a woman so much as smiled at him?

Nobody made him leave the party with Greeley. Nobody asked him to drive her pickup or take her to his hotel. Nobody asked him to come to Aspen and shove himself into her life. Nobody asked him to force Greeley to meet Fern. Whatever had happened last night—and nothing had—it was on his head.

Not hers. She would never have gone to bed with him. His theatrical subterfuge to frighten her away had been totally unnecessary. She didn't hop into bed with strange men to solve her problems. And if she did, she certainly wouldn't hop into bed with Quint Damian, so he needn't think he was some kind of Greek god she idolized. She couldn't stand him.

Giving the metal one last good solid whack, Greeley stood back to study the work in progress. Arrogant, egotistical bull elk. Thought all elk cows were hot for him when the females just wanted to be left alone to live their lives.

The ringing phone sliced through the quiet afternoon.

Quint's grandfather was on the other end. "Edward Damian," he said. "We met in passing last night."

As if she could have forgotten.

"Fern feels terrible about last night. She was so shocked she didn't know what she was doing. I don't know how she managed to stay at the party, but she's a trouper. She insisted it would be rude to leave."

As Greeley had left. Score one for Fern.

"Mr. Damian, there's no point in you trying to talk me into going to Denver."

"I'm not." His surprise came clearly over the wires. "Quint explained to me how it would be a very bad idea. I'm real sorry. If I'd known about your fragile mental state, I'd never have sent him after you."

It was Greeley's turn to be surprised. "My what?"

"I had no idea you were prone to bouts of excitability. Quint says you need to be handled with kid gloves, on account of how sensitive and delicate you are, and he pointed out a couple of rough and rugged guys like us don't know beans about dealing with an emotional, easily bruised young woman like yourself. Naturally, your mother's disappointed, but she doesn't want to risk your health. Maybe when you're a little older, we can have dinner together or something. If you're feeling up to it, of course," he added quickly.

Greeley unclenched her teeth and spoke decisively into the phone.

"Well?" Quint demanded of his grandfather.

Big Ed put down the phone and grinned. "You were right. She went for it, hook, line and sinker. She'll meet you in front the hotel at nine o'clock tomorrow morning and stay with us in Denver until the wedding." He looked at his watch. "I promised Fern I'd take her shopping. I better get going."

Quint watched absently as his grandfather went out the door.

Fern hadn't exactly embraced the idea of Greeley returning to Denver with them, but Granddad's enthusiasm had given her little choice but to agree. Fern probably felt safe in assuming Greeley would refuse.

If forced to bet, Quint's thinking would have paralleled Fern's. Not that anything was set in stone. Once her irritation wore off, Greeley would certainly realize she'd been manipulated into agreeing. What would happen then was anybody's guess.

From the beginning, Greeley Lassiter had reacted in ways that defied Quint's best efforts to anticipate. Or manage.

He saw his current dilemma as two-sided. Granddad still had to be brought face-to-face with Fern's true nature, and Quint had to repair any damage he might have done to Greeley. Bringing the two women together would solve both his problems, he hoped.

Granddad would quickly pick up on Fern's lack of interest in her daughter. He'd know Fern had lied and wonder what else she'd lied about.

As for Greeley, she'd be forced to confront the differences and similarities between herself and her mother. Greeley could decide for herself if she was like Fern. If she was…Quint shrugged. He was off the hook. No guilt, no blame. He wouldn't care what happened to Fern's daughter.

If Greeley wasn't like her mother, the truth would be self-evident. She could forget all her nonsense about bad blood.

And Quint might be able to forget he was the conniving bully who'd forced her to confront her mother, and smashed her dreams. He could put the entire fiasco behind him.

If Greeley showed up at nine in the morning.

Quint pulled into a long driveway leading to a large, sprawling, one-story, beige brick house. Greeley parked behind his sports car and looked around. Massive old pine, spruce and juniper trees bordered a green carpet of lawn around the house, giving the yard the appearance of a private park.

Artfully placed flower beds burst with a colorful profusion of roses, daisies, petunias, columbines and foxgloves. Frenzied barking came from the back of the house as she stepped from her truck.

Quint lifted her suitcases from the bed of the pickup. "Here we are," he said unnecessarily. A brick walk led the way to the front door. The barking rose in pitch to a frantic howling. "Pipe down," Quint yelled. The dog redoubled its efforts.

Inside the house, Quint mumbled something about neighbors and noise and disappeared toward the back of the house.

The cavernous living room with multiple brown leather seating brought to mind an exclusive men's club. At the far end of the room a light-colored brick fireplace rose to the ceiling. Dark wooden shelves on either side of the fireplace held dozens of photographs and metal trophies. Greeley moved closer. Starting from the left, the photos documented a boy's life. Baby, toddler, adolescent. The youth might have been a younger Quint, if not for the clothing, which came from an earlier era.

A high-school diploma read, "Edward Quinton Damian, Jr." The same name appeared on the commission in the air force which hung below a college diploma from the Air Force Academy. A photograph showed a young man who greatly resembled Quint wearing a military uniform.

The final frame held a newspaper obituary from the late 1960s.

Greeley went back and inspected the trophies. Football, golf, softball. All the inscriptions read "Eddie Damian."

"My father."

She hadn't heard him return. "I assumed. I'm not as stupid as you think I am. The minute I hung up the phone I realized your grandfather had herded me like a dumb cow into exactly the pen he wanted me in." She stood in front of a shelf displaying medals. "What's all this?"

"My father's pilot's wings, first lieutenant bars, National

Defense Service Medal, air medals, medals issued by the Republic of Vietnam, a Purple Heart and the Air Force Cross.''

"What's the Air Force Cross for?"

"For being a hero. He was co-pilot on a 130 cargo plane that got shot up landing at Da Nang and came in with an engine on fire. They had ammo on board, so the pilot yelled at everyone to get out fast. When my father reached safety, he realized the pilot and crew chief were still on board, so he went back. The pilot had a broken leg, but my father pulled him out and returned for the crew chief. The plane blew up with him and the crew chief on board.'' Quint recited the stark details in a detached voice, before asking, "Why did you come if you think Granddad was manipulating you?"

She refused to feel sorry for him. Or acknowledge the shadows in his eyes when he talked about his father. "All my life people have made my decisions for me. Pushed and pulled and put me where they wanted. Played with my life. It's time I did a little playing with theirs."

"Revenge," he said evenly.

"Don't be melodramatic. I couldn't pass up the opportunity to get to know my birth mother, could I?" She gave Quint a glittery smile. "We have so many things to tell each other."

"You're naive if you expect Fern to clasp you to her maternal bosom.''

Greeley rounded her eyes in a parody of innocence. "You think she'll be worried sick I'll spill the beans to your grandfather about how I ended up at the Double Nickel? Or do you think Fern won't want around an adult daughter, who's not only a reminder of her wicked youth, but of passing time?"

He gave her a curious look. "You've decided to sabotage her plans to marry Granddad?"

"I want to show her I'm no longer a tiny helpless bundle

in a blanket.'' She waited a beat. ''Then I plan to do all in my power to make sure nothing—and nobody—stands in the way of her marrying your grandfather.''

''Why? What's it to you who she marries?''

''It's nothing to me.'' She emphasized the pronoun.

His jaw tightened. ''Let me guess. You're playing the woman scorned. Forget it. You didn't want to fall into bed with me any more than I wanted to fall into bed with you.''

A warm flush crawled up her face. ''This has nothing to do with that.'' At his derisive look, she said heatedly, ''You're entirely to blame for what happened the other night. You burst into my life and demanded I do your bidding. I told you repeatedly I didn't want to meet Fern, but that didn't stop you. Ignoring my wishes, you forced a meeting on me.'' Greeley glared at him. ''I wasn't a person to you. Just a tool you could use. To heck with the consequences for me. All that counted was what Quint Damian wanted. Okay, maybe I did go a little crazy and act like a fool the other night. You were willing enough to take advantage of my state of mind.''

''I didn't take advantage of you.''

''Only because I left before you could.'' She refused to admit she knew he'd deliberately engineered her escape.

''If anyone was trying to take advantage of anyone, just remember whose idea it was to have sex.''

Greeley raised her chin. ''You can't use my behavior to force me to do what you want.'' Turning her back to him, she stared at his father's medals. ''You had no qualms about turning my life upside down. Now I'm going to turn yours upside down. We'll see how you like it.''

He wanted to run his fingers down her unyielding spine. Wanted to kiss those arrogant, defiant lips until they softened and kissed him back.

He'd made a mishmash of this entire situation. Kissing Fern's daughter would only make matters worse.

Barney scratched furiously at the closed door to the

kitchen. He'd wolfed down the food Quint had bribed him with and wanted into the living room. "Do you mind if I let Barney in?" The dog could distract Greeley while Quint considered this latest wrinkle in his plans.

"Of course not," she said coolly. "You said he was a trained guard dog."

That wasn't exactly what he'd said. Implied, maybe. "He did go to obedience school." The second Quint cracked open the door, Barney wiggled through and tore across the room to investigate their visitor, his tail wagging his entire rear end. "He didn't exactly graduate with honors."

Greeley looked in disbelief at the beagle bouncing excitedly around her feet. "I thought you found a guard dog at the animal shelter."

Quint hated looking ridiculous. He fixed his eyes on Barney's squirming body. "Yeah, well, when I went to the animal shelter, the first dog I saw was Barney. Electronic security at Damian Trucking makes more sense anyway."

She dropped to her knees, looking about sixteen in her blue jeans and white knit shirt, her hair hanging down her back in a fat braid. "He's sweet." Her laughter rang out as the beagle washed her face with his tongue.

Quint hadn't heard her laugh before. Not like this. Carefree peals of laughter. She should laugh more often. "Just push him away. Granddad spoils him rotten."

She gave Quint a teasing, enchanting smile. "But you, of course, don't spoil him."

Her smiles ought to come with a label warning of their dangerous impact on a man's midsection. And lower.

"What was a sweet little guy like you doing in the pound?" she crooned, scratching behind Barney's long ears.

If she scratched and fondled him, Quint would pant, too. Greeley looked expectantly at him. He had to quit visualizing her in his bed. "His owner died. A man about eighty-five. There wasn't anyone to take Barney. I couldn't let him be put down," he added defensively.

"Softy. What other deep, dark secrets are you hiding?"

More than she'd ever know. "I'll put you in Mom's rooms. You should have everything you need there."

"Where is your mother?" She followed him down the long hall, Barney shadowing her footsteps.

All traces of her earlier anger seemed to have evaporated with Barney's appearance. Or been temporarily set aside. Quint gratefully accepted what he felt sure would be a short truce. "Albuquerque. She married a former sweetheart she ran into at their high-school class's twentieth reunion." Jan Damian had been reluctant to accept Phil's proposal, but she'd carried her first husband's burden for eighteen years, and Quint had convinced her it was time she passed the torch to him. He'd been doing fine until Fern came along.

"Where's Fern staying?"

"Big Ed has the other wing." Let her figure out the obvious. "When Mom moved in with me, she and Granddad set up some ground rules. Mom and I in our wing, Granddad in his, and the main section of the house sort of public territory. With Mom helping out at the company, that gave them each some private space. Granddad and I saw no reason to change the arrangement when Mom moved out."

"I think I ought to sleep in the other wing."

"No room." Passing through his mother's sitting room to the bedroom, he set Greeley's suitcases on the bed. "Worried you'll be tempted to sneak into my bed?"

"Of course not."

She had beautiful eyes. Eyes filled with an edgy awareness of him and the sexual attraction which hovered between them. Quint couldn't resist running a finger down the side of her face. "Then you must be scared I'll be tempted to sneak into your bed."

"You don't scare me."

He scared himself.

He wanted to grab her chin and plaster kisses all over her defiant face. Make love to her until she wiggled as ecstatically under his hands as Barney had under hers. Cupping her cheek with his hand, he pressed his palm against her soft, warm skin.

If he kissed her, here, now, he wouldn't be able to stop. It would only take a second to shove her suitcases from the bed.

His mother's bed. Quint thought of promises made and kept. A promise given by son to mother. By wife to husband. The promise he'd made to his mother on the day she married Phil. Remembering, he walked out of the bedroom.

Away from Fern's daughter.

It wasn't as if Greeley wanted him to kiss her. She wasn't disappointed he hadn't.

Maybe he thought the threat of a kiss would frighten her into abandoning her plan to cross him. He thought wrong. She would not be intimidated by childish charades and threatening innuendos. If Quint Damian wanted to convey a tough-guy image, he needed to get a different dog.

The sheepish look on his face when Barney burst into the living room had been sweet and kind of appealing.

Greeley mentally slapped herself. One tiny soft spot in a man's cold metal heart didn't make him a selfless philanthropist. Quint Damian was still the man who put his financial gain ahead of his grandfather's happiness. Who sacrificed anyone and everyone in his selfish, grasping drive to own his grandfather's business.

Greeley yanked at one of the zippers on her suitcase. Her time would be better spent unpacking instead of thinking about kisses she didn't want.

The first drawer she opened held baby pictures. Someone had carefully labeled them on the back. Quint had been bald the first six months of his life. A cocky five-year-old. Missing teeth at seven. So proud at ten in his softball uniform. Tall and skinny the first day of high school. Awkward and self-conscious in a tuxedo before a high-school dance.

He'd begun filling out in college. Wider shoulders. A deeper chest. The five-year-old's cockiness had been become a young man's self-assurance.

The masculine power and controlled sensuality must have come later.

Putting the photographs back in the drawer, Greeley slammed it shut.

The sound of Barney whining and scratching led Greeley to the back of the house. The beagle fussed on one side of a glass door, adding to the canine nose prints covering the bottom of the door. A piece of paper taped to the door said, "Don't let dog in pool room."

Greeley peered through the glass. Assorted plants and wicker furniture lined a long room glassed on three sides. A lap pool ran down the center of the room. In the pool, Quint stroked through the water, the muscles in his arms and shoulders flexing powerfully with each deliberate stroke. At the far end of the pool, he executed an underwater turn and began another lap. His wet shoulders gleamed as the afternoon sun penetrated the glass walls.

Greeley wondered how many laps he swam. How much time she had to search for the answers to some questions.

She headed back down the hall.

Quint's room was almost monastic in its simplicity. An old-fashioned iron bed with a forest-green cover. Straight green hangings at the windows. A black leather chair with matching footstool and a modern chrome reading light.

Barney trotted into the room and made for a plump dog bed in the corner. Head on the bed's edge he watched Greeley until his eyes slowly closed.

"Some guard dog you are," she said softly, her words drowned out by his snores.

Two large posters advertising Damian Trucking hung on one wall. Looking at the trucks pictured, Greeley judged the posters dated from the 1940s.

Silver-framed photographs marched with military precision across the top of a sturdy, medium-brown oak chest of drawers. Greeley recognized Quint's father in a wedding photo. Quint's mother was an attractive woman who bore little resemblance to her adult son.

Except for the color of her gray-green eyes. Greeley studied the woman in the colored wedding picture. Her eyes held humor and warmth and brimmed with love. Kind eyes. Pleasant.

Not cool and judgmental.

Or heated and sensual.

There were no pictures of Quint in the room.

His father again. In some kind of uniform this time, standing by a plane. He held a flight helmet.

Greeley picked up another photograph. A different military man. The same age, but from another era, another war. Quint's grandfather, she guessed. Another frame held medals and a small brass plaque with Edward Damian's name.

The last picture was another wedding photo. Quint's mother, older, but looking too young to have an adult son. The web of age lines around her eyes took away nothing from her attractiveness. If anything, she'd matured into greater beauty. Or maybe that was the warm glow of happiness in her eyes.

If her new husband had ever had the striking male arrogance of the Damian males, age had tempered it. He looked kind and pleasant. Generous. Greeley wondered what he thought of his selfish, self-centered stepson. She set the photograph back on the chest.

"Find what you're looking for?"

Greeley jumped. "Don't sneak up on me like that."

"You were so busy snooping, an eighteen-wheeler could have come down the hall and you wouldn't have heard it."

"If parts of the house are off-limits, you should have told me." She turned. A mistake. Quint leaned against the side of his doorway, a white towel wrapped around his hips, his arms crossed in front of his bare chest. His shoulders looked wider without clothes. He must swim a lot to build those kind of muscles in his arms and chest. She licked suddenly dry lips. "Enjoy your swim?"

He raised an eyebrow. "I wondered why Barney quit yapping at me. He followed you back here."

"Why can't he go in the pool room?"

"Too hard for him to get out of the pool with his short legs and squat body." He pushed away from the door jamb. "You didn't answer my question. Find what you were looking for?"

"No."

"That's because I cleverly keep gold bars and diamonds in a family vault deep in the earth."

"Very amusing."

"What *were* you looking for?"

"You."

He gave an exaggerated glance around the room. "Even if you didn't see me in the pool, where do you suppose I could have been hiding in here?"

Greeley knew all about hiding. "There's no pictures of you. No trophies, no scrapbooks, no mementos."

"So?" He pulled open a chest drawer.

"I'm looking for what makes you tick. So I can find your weak spots."

"What makes you think I have any?"

"Everybody does."

"What are yours?"

Sanity took hold before she could say, "Green eyes." Instead she said, "We've already discussed my failings."

"Somehow I doubt it." He opened a door across the room and waved his hand at a huge expanse of walk-in closet. "My junk's in here. Be my guest. I'm going to take a hot shower."

When he emerged, fully dressed, from the steamy bathroom, Greeley sat curled up in the middle of his bed, a high-school yearbook across her lap. Barney lay beside her, his head on her knee, his eyes closed. She looked as if she belonged there. Quint knew she didn't.

Neither did Barney. "You're not supposed to be on the bed," Quint said sternly.

The dog opened one eye, looked at him, and closed the eye.

Greeley turned a page. "Unless you were talking to me, he's not very well trained."

"He's trained well enough when other people aren't spoiling him."

"First your grandfather, now me." She turned another page, then turned the book sideways, reading a hand-written message. "Whoa, Missy sure had the hots for you, didn't she? Along with Heather and Jessica and Wendy and Sarah and I can't remember who else. I don't know how you had time to play football and be in the drama club and get good grades."

"It was high school. Ancient history."

"Most likely to succeed. Have you?"

He took the yearbook from her. "I paid everybody to vote for me." Gathering up the other books, he carried them back into the closet. His box of trophies sat on the floor. He put the box back up on the top shelf and dragged the footstool back where it belonged. "I thought you'd be snooping in your mother's room instead of in here." He'd prefer her anywhere but here, lying on his bed, her head on his pillow, her arms folded behind her head.

He wanted to move Barney and lay his own head on her thigh.

"If you mean Fern, it wouldn't be fair to go through her things."

"But it's okay to snoop through mine?"

"Fern didn't know she was going to meet me. Didn't know I would be coming back here. It would be like unexpectedly walking in on someone bare naked in the shower."

He'd thought about her bare naked in his shower while he'd been showering. What was it about this woman that she twisted his insides into a knot without her even trying? Unless she *was* trying. No woman was that innocent. Lying there in a provocative pose on his bed. Choosing words meant to torment him.

She was still talking. "It would be taking unfair advantage, like sneaking up on her."

"I take it you have no problems sneaking up on me?"

Greeley gave him a look of exaggerated surprise. "How could I be sneaking when you practically dragged me to Denver? All's fair in love and war." She immediately blushed at her own words.

Quint resisted the temptation to pounce on them. Or on her. He moved toward the bedroom door. "I have work to do, so I'll leave you to your prying."

She sat up. "That's your grandfather, isn't it?" She pointed to the photo she'd guessed was Big Ed. When he nodded, she asked, "How come you didn't join the military?"

"Didn't interest me. Didn't really interest Big Ed, but he was drafted. He was a POW for two years."

"Is that what the medals were for?"

"No. He held off the enemy until the rest of his platoon got away. He wouldn't have been caught but he got shot up."

"Your family is just loaded with heroes, isn't it?"

Quint's insides seized up. "I'll be in the office in Granddad's wing." He escaped before she could ask where his medals were.

Greeley would give anything if she could take back her taunting words. No matter how Beau had hurt and angered her, she'd always been proud of his accomplishments and his trophy belt buckles. Belt buckles paled beside saving men's lives. Quint had every reason to be proud of his father and grandfather. Mocking them and sneering at their deeds showed a side of herself Greeley didn't like.

"He drives me crazy," she said to Barney.

The dog opened his eyes and stretched. If he could talk, he'd no doubt tell her they both knew she couldn't blame Quint for her unacceptable behavior.

Greeley nudged him. "Come on, Barney. We'd better get off his bed and go apologize." Standing, she took one last long look around the room. Either Quint Damian had nothing to hide or he knew more about hiding than Greeley did.

She doubted it was the former.

Barney took off down the hall. Greeley followed. The dog would know where to find Quint.

CHAPTER SIX

GREELEY TRAILED after Barney toward the sound of Quint's voice. He sat with his back to her, his feet propped on the windowsill, a phone cradled between his head and his shoulder. "Yeah, I'll explain. Sure, I understand."

Barney padded into the office, and Quint glanced over his shoulder to where Greeley stood pretending not to eavesdrop. His steady gaze on her, he listened to the person on the other end of the line. "Yeah, okay, see you then."

The way Quint hung up the phone, devoting entirely too much attention to the mundane task, told Greeley the conversation affected her.

He lowered his legs and turned his chair toward her. "That was my grandfather."

"They at the Denver International Airport?"

Avoiding her gaze, he said. "At lunch they ran into this movie producer they met at Cheyenne's party. The man invited them to a party. Granddad thought he ought to attend. For business reasons. Film crews need a lot of stuff moved when they go on location." Quint fiddled with a pencil on his desk. "The producer's going to fly them back to DIA after the party."

He looked braced for an explosion. As if he expected to be blamed for Fern not rushing to see her precious daughter. Greeley wasn't stupid enough to believe Fern cared about her one way or the other. Greeley hadn't come to Denver to forge any bonds with Fern. She'd come to make mischief, plain and simple. "I assume Fern went with your grandfather."

"What do you think?" Quint asked, more than a hint of anger in his voice. "If you've seen any indication that your mother is dying to get acquainted with her long-lost daughter, you have more imagination than I do. If anything, she's staying as far away from you as she can.''

Greeley didn't bother to argue. She knew he was right. ''I suppose they'll be pretty late.''

''Pretty late.'' Quint bounced the pencil on its eraser end. ''Granddad called from L.A. The party's on Maui.''

''In Hawaii?''

''Unless they moved it.''

''But they can't possibly make it back here tonight.''

''No.'' A heartbeat of silence passed. ''Is that a problem?''

Of course it was a problem. She couldn't spend the night in this house alone with him. So much for her grand plan to show everyone what it felt like to stand helplessly by while others messed with your life. Fern had thwarted that plan before Greeley had hardly begun. She'd been a fool to come to Denver, and the sooner she left, the better. ''I didn't bring much. It won't take me long to pack.''

''No. Stay. They could be back tomorrow. After all, they have a wedding in less than two weeks.''

''You know they won't be back tomorrow. They're in Maui. Who would leave Maui after one night?''

''You'd have to turn right around and come back for the wedding.''

''I wouldn't have to come at all.''

''What happened to your grand scheme for revenge?''

''It wasn't about revenge. It was about teaching people they couldn't act like little tin gods, interfering in other people's lives for selfish and whimsical reasons.''

''Okay, what about that?''

Greeley grimaced. ''I'm clearly outclassed. Coming to Denver was a waste of time and gasoline.''

''It doesn't have to be,'' Quint said slowly. ''You could accept a commission to sculpt something for Granddad. Something large to go in front of Damian Trucking. Come down to the terminal with me tomorrow. Check out the nuts and bolts of our trucking operation. Talk to some of the drivers. See what we do, how we operate. Climb around our trucks. You're bound to get plenty of good ideas for a sculpture.''

Greeley gave him a disgusted look. "Forget it. Commissioning a work from me won't persuade me to break up your grandfather's romance with Fern.''

"Do you always allow personal considerations to influence your career decisions? No wonder women have trouble being taken seriously in the business world.''

She tamped down rising irritation. "You're insulting me with gender-based stereotypes because you can't deny the truth of what I said.''

"You wouldn't believe me if I did deny it. Do you have so little confidence in your work that you can't believe I'd see something you've done and want you to make something for me?''

The question poked too close to the truth. The terror invoked by publicly exhibiting her statues, submitting them for criticism, and offering them for sale was the stuff of nightmares. "That's not the point," she said defensively.

Satisfaction gleamed in his eyes. Her answer had been too weak. He thought he was going to get what he wanted. Greeley bristled. "I'm not going to waste time and energy on a commission you have no intention of paying for. I can always sell horses, but I doubt there's a big demand for truck sculptures.''

Quint opened a desk drawer and withdrew a piece of paper. "We'll write up a contract. A deposit from me up front, balance due upon completion of the sculpture.''

"You mean you'll pay the balance due if I convince your grandfather that Fern is the woman you think she is, but if I support Fern marrying him, you'll claim you don't like the sculpture and badmouth me up and down the Rocky Mountains and destroy what little reputation I have as an artist.''

He eyed her thoughtfully. "You're not a very trusting person, are you?"

"Being abandoned as a baby teaches a person real quick you can't count on anyone," she retorted.

"I have a feeling Mary Lassiter would take issue with that self-pitying statement."

Greeley felt her face warm. "You don't care what you say as long as you get your own way, do you?"

"Do you always try to pick a fight with potential patrons?"

"It's a free country. I can turn down a commission if I want. Especially one as dubious as yours."

"Why would you want to turn it down? A large, important commission for a commercial client with all the accompanying hoopla in the Denver newspapers, the art pages as well as the business pages. Cheyenne said you need to introduce yourself to the Denver art scene. A sculpture for Damian Trucking could do that."

"I don't—"

"What are you afraid of? Failure?" He paused. "Or something more basic? Such as whether you trust yourself alone here with me."

"Don't be ridiculous. I have no personal interest in you whatsoever."

"Good. Then you'll stay." He shoved the blank sheet of paper toward her. "Write out a contract and I'll sign it."

"I don't...trucks aren't exactly my usual..." Her voice died away. He was right about one thing. Turning down a commission like this without taking time to consider it would be foolish.

"Think how you'd impress Davy."

She almost smiled. "That would be an important consideration, of course."

The look on his face said he thought he'd won. He hadn't. She pushed the paper back. "I'll go down to your truck place tomorrow and look around, but I'm not committing to anything.'' Staying one night, going with him tomorrow, changed nothing.

He couldn't manipulate her into coming between Fern and his grandfather. He couldn't persuade her to do his bidding.

He couldn't charm his way into her bed.

Quint opened the blinds wider to improve his view.

''What's so interesting out there?'' Beth walked into the office.

''Nothing. You find the Beckwell contract?''

''Yes. It's on your desk.'' His secretary joined him in front of the large window overlooking the yard. ''She doesn't look like nothing to me. She looks like trouble.''

''You'd think anyone who'd worked for Damian Trucking as long as you have would remember who's the boss and who's hired help.''

Beth ignored his sarcasm. ''You showing up with Fern's daughter this morning sure turned this place on its ear.''

''I brought her because she's interested in trucks and our operation here.'' If Quint even hinted he'd commissioned Greeley to make a sculpture for his grandfather, word would get back to Big Ed quicker than Barney could gobble down his dinner. ''She wouldn't have turned anything on its ear if my employees attended to business and did what they are paid to do.''

''Imagine having Fern for a mother-in-law.''

A muscle jumped in his jaw. ''The question doesn't arise.''

''Good. You can do better than Fern's daughter. It wouldn't work anyway. She'd be bound to resent a man taking up with her after her mother dumped him. Not that I believed for one second Fern dumped you instead of the other way around.''

''I didn't dump Fern,'' Quint said tightly. ''We had a few business dinners. As when Jack and I go to dinner.''

''Uh-huh. When was the last time Jack kissed you?''

So much for hoping Beth hadn't seen that kiss. ''Fern

slipped on a piece of ice and I caught her.'' He'd tried to tell himself she was hanging on his arm to keep from falling, that she didn't know her breasts pressed around his arm. She'd laughed at the near fall and when he'd looked down at her, she'd kissed him on the mouth.

His evident shock had elicited a quick, embarrassed apology from her. She'd meant to give him a grateful kiss on his cheek, but he'd turned his head.... He'd accepted her explanation and quelled his suspicions.

Later he'd learned Fern was spreading word around the office that they were dating. He'd immediately called her into his office and baldly told her they were not dating and would not be dating.

Fern had retaliated by latching on to Big Ed, digging her talons into him so securely, Quint's grandfather refused to listen to any warnings from his grandson. Quint had come off looking like a rejected, jealous boyfriend.

A jealous boyfriend was the last thing he'd been. Fern interviewed well, had seemed pleasant and capable, and he'd hired her, believing she'd be an asset to the front office. He hadn't been sexually attracted to her.

Which made being attracted to her daughter all the more perplexing. And irksome.

After his dealings with Fern, the last woman who should interest him was the woman standing on the semi-tractor's step, leaning into the cab.

Greeley Lassiter wasn't his type. She was too extreme, too detached, too emotional. Her moods ranged all over the map. A man never knew what to expect. An ice maiden or a red-hot, sexy bombshell.

Like now. Her jeans fit so tightly they looked like a second skin of blue denim, covering a firm, rounded bottom—a bottom a man's fingers itched to touch. She ought to know better than to run around in provocative, sexy clothes stirring up the hormones of his mechanics.

"What do you suppose she and Jack are finding so fascinating to talk about?" Beth asked.

Since Jack was Damian Trucking's shop supervisor, Quint could answer with complete certainty. "They're talking engines, what else?"

"Quint dated Fern?" Greeley asked in disbelief. "You've got to be kidding. She's old enough to be his mother."

"I wouldn't go that far," Jack said. "Quint's thirty-one, and Beth said Fern's only in her mid-forties. You got to admit, she's aged well. Besides, they weren't exactly dating. Quint works hard, long hours. Many's the time him and me grabbed a burger somewhere so we could discuss something or other. Easier to talk business after hours without the phones ringing and customers coming in. After hours usually means dinnertime."

Quint Damian didn't strike Greeley as the kind of man who was so naive he couldn't distinguish between a business dinner and a date. "You said Fern dated Quint before she dated his grandfather."

Jack shook his head. "I said Fern took up with Big Ed because Quint quit taking her out to dinner. According to Beth, once Quint heard the office gossip about him and Fern, he called Fern into his office. Beth couldn't hear what was said, but right after that Fern told everyone she dumped Quint because he was shallow and immature and she preferred older men."

He shook his head again. "Big Ed's been a bachelor for almost fifty years. Plenty of women have tried to change that status, but he had Eddie Junior, and then Quint and his mama. Jan, she remarried and moved out twelve years ago, and I guess Big Ed figured Quint would find a woman one of these days." Jack peered at Greeley from under bushy eyebrows. "Not that Quint would ever leave his granddaddy. There's plenty of room in that old house. You don't need to worry Big Ed'll be in your hair."

Startled, Greeley lost her balance and almost fell into the cab. "I'm not going to live with Fern and Mr. Damian."

"Fern." Jack spat on the ground. "I was talking about you and Quint living with the old man."

Astonished by the shop supervisor's incredible assumption, Greeley ignored Barney's barked greeting and hastened to set the shop supervisor straight. "Quint and I aren't dating. I don't even like him. He's the most selfish, self-involved man I've ever met."

Jack's astonishment mirrored hers. "Quint? Selfish? What do you smoke down there in Aspen?"

"Doesn't anybody work around this place anymore?"

Greeley jumped as Quint's voice cracked through the air behind her. Turning, she leaned back against the door frame. "Don't yell at Jack. You told him to show me around and answer any questions I had."

Quint's eyes narrowed. "Obviously I should have been more specific about those questions."

"Obviously you should have told Jack why I'm here. I don't appreciate being lumped in with the harebrained women you date."

"Maybe I'll go see how the guys are coming along with that transmission they're pulling," Jack said.

"You do that," Quint said coldly. "It'd be nice if somebody around here earned his salary," he added to Jack's departing back.

"I might have known you'd be snotty to your employees," Greeley said in a caustic voice. "I don't know how anyone can stand to work for you."

"Jack's been here almost forty years."

"He's either a saint or he's putting up with you for your grandfather's sake." She crossed her arms in front of her chest. "Which is more than I intend to do."

"Would you care to elaborate on that statement?"

He couldn't intimidate her with a haughty, overbearing tone of voice. Not after the way he'd manipulated her. Again.

She glared down at him. "You have no intention of buying a sculpture from me. You lied so I'd stay in Denver while you figured out how to trick me into breaking up your grandfather's romance with your ex-girlfriend. You're incensed about Fern marrying him because you're jealous."

"I'm not jealous and she's not my ex-girlfriend," he said, hardly moving his taut jaw.

"Your problem is you're not looking at the big picture," Greeley jeered. "Instead of acting like a spurned lover, you ought to be patient. Once your grandfather dies, you can marry Fern and get the entire business back so you can pass it on to your children." Through talking to him, she stepped down from the truck to walk away.

Quint moved quickly. One second he stood two arm lengths away, the next second, his hands were pressed against the semi, one arm on either side of her, corralling her. The sudden move caught Greeley off-balance, and she clutched at his upper arms to stabilize herself. The slick, ironed shirt sleeves covered hard, powerful muscles.

"I have no intention of marrying Fern Kelly," he said coldly. "For many reasons, not the least of which is I wouldn't want any of my children carrying so much as a drop of her blood."

He stood too close, but Greeley refused to back away. Not that she could. Not with the semi-tractor pressing against her back. All too conscious of his wide shoulders and broad chest, she forced herself to concentrate on his insult. "Maybe you ought to put that tidbit on the employee bulletin board."

"What's that supposed to mean?"

"Fern's blood runs in me, and your employees are madly speculating on our relationship. Everyone here thinks we're...that we have a personal interest in each other. They think we're sleeping together. Half of them probably have us going down the aisle."

It wasn't too much of an exaggeration. If Quint's shop supervisor thought so, the rest of Quint's employees undoubtedly did, too. Anger ran deep in her. Along with the tiniest tinge of regret. Although what she regretted, she couldn't imagine.

"Don't be ridiculous," Quint said curtly. "I'm not going to marry you or sleep with you."

Regret vanished in a flash. "I'm well aware you're only interested in using me to pay back Fern for dumping you."

"Fern did not dump me."

Greeley gave him a highly skeptical look. "It must be tough being dumped for your own grandfather," she said in a mocking voice. "Having to endure the sideways glances, the whispers over the water cooler...."

"You want whispers over the water cooler?" Quint asked in a furious voice. "I'll give you whispers." He hauled her up against his chest and pressed a hard mouth against hers.

Greeley went stiff as a board. She didn't want him kissing her because he'd been rejected by her birth mother. She wouldn't be a substitute for Fern. The semi was hard and hot against her back. The scent of warm rubber and diesel fuel stung her nose.

After a second, Quint raised his head. "How do you do that?" His grip eased, but he didn't release her. "You drive me so crazy I forget everything I ever learned about how to treat a woman. From the first minute I saw you in the Gilded Lily at the St. Christopher Hotel, I've had this inexplicable urge to reduce everything between us to the most basic, rawest, sexual level." His fingers tightened at her waist. "You must fling some kind of magic, instant-lust powder in my face."

The words, his deepened voice, had a powerful effect on her stomach. Greeley didn't like the feeling. "I don't want you to kiss me." She studied a button on his pale green shirt.

"Not like that. How do you feel if I kiss you like this?"

No one could resist lips which teased and nibbled. Clinging to his arms, Greeley parted her lips under his persuasive mouth and instantly went weak in the knees as he slid his tongue over hers. Her eyes shut tight, she concentrated on learning the nuances of his mouth and sharing the secrets of hers. The sharp, biting odors of the terminal faded away to be replaced by his exciting, masculine scent. Her insides took off on a wild, stomach-dropping, mind-bending roller-coaster ride.

When he'd reduced her to a formless lump of need and desire, Quint slowly raised his head. "Well?"

"Well, what?" He expected her to be able to think after he'd kissed her like that?

"Did you like that better?"

Greeley had never understood what smoldering eyes meant until she looked into his. More gray than green. Dark and hazy with swirling currents of heat and desire. Charcoal embers on the verge of bursting into flame.

She wanted to warm herself in their heat.

Before she could betray herself, she looked away, glancing down. Barney sat on his haunches, his head cocked to one side, curiosity on his face as he gazed up at them. A weak giggle caught in Greeley's throat. Quint's dog couldn't be any more amazed than she was. "Barney thinks we're nuts."

With one hand Quint braced himself against the semi-tractor. "We are." He slid his other hand slowly down her hip. "Certifiably."

She wanted to edge away from his hand. Her body wanted to melt into it. A siren song of unimaginable pleasures sang in her ears, tempting her to fling caution to the winds.

Common sense prevailed. Sexual attraction meant nothing without love. And love had nothing to do with what happened when Quint kissed her. "When I see you, I don't have an urge to, well, whatever you have an urge to do. I usually want to strangle you." There was some truth in her words.

"That's because chemical attraction rises slower in women."

"Is that something you learned in basic biology?" Greeley asked tartly.

Quint smiled and raised a hand to brush a wisp of hair away from her face. "You're really something. It's too bad..."

Greeley had no trouble finishing his abandoned sentence. "...too bad I'm related to Fern," she said coolly. She refused to be hurt by his holding against her Fern's sins. "You should have remembered my bad blood before you put on an exhibition for your employees."

"You kissed me back."

"Maybe I wanted to see to what depths you'd sink to get your own way. Letting everyone here think you're interested in me when you're only interested in using me." She used his lies to whip up her anger. Anger was far better than hurt. "That's lying to them as much as you've been lying to me."

"I told you up front I wanted you to come to Denver and cure my grandfather of this ridiculous infatuation he has for Fern."

"I'm not talking about that. I'm talking about the sculpture. There's not one person here at Damian Trucking who knows anything about you commissioning me to make sculpture for your grandfather."

"You didn't tell someone about the truck sculpture?"

The dismay in his voice erased any lingering doubts. "No, and neither did you. Why is that? Because the commission is a total sham, isn't it?"

"I didn't tell anyone the real reason you're to have free access to all aspects of our operation because I want the sculpture to be a surprise birthday gift for Granddad, and there is no such thing as a secret around here. Since you appear to have heard every little detail of Fern's kissing me, you should know that by now."

Greeley stared at him in shock. Jack had talked about dinners. He'd said nothing about kisses. The thought of Quint kissing Fern in the same way he'd kissed Greeley nauseated her. "You kissed Fern? Did you sleep with her, too?"

Quint exhaled loudly and took one step back, running a

hand through his hair. "I did not kiss Fern. She kissed me. There is a world of difference."

Greeley paid no attention to the photographs lining the wall in front of her. Her mind was locked on an internal image of Fern and Quint locked in each other's arms. Not that their May-December romance interested her. Except that Quint should have told her the real reason he opposed Fern marrying his grandfather.

A desk drawer slammed behind her. "Is there something I can help you with?" Quint's secretary asked in a voice which bordered on rude.

"No, thank you, Mrs. Curtis. I just came in to get away from the noise and smell of the shop." To get away from Quint. Every time she watched a repair, or transmission work, or an electrical system being tested, Quint appeared at her side. As if guarding his male employees from her. Obviously she posed no danger to his female staff.

Beth Curtis sniffed. "Your mother doesn't like going in the shop either. Of course, she doesn't know a wrench from a voltmeter. I don't suppose you do either."

Greeley saw no reason to tell Quint's secretary she probably knew more about diesel engines than Quint Damian, with his freshly laundered, immaculately pressed shirts, would ever know.

Facing the wall, she pretended interest in the photographs. A group of teenagers wearing baseball uniforms grinned broadly for the camera. Quint and one of the mechanics she'd met earlier stood in the back. No longer faking interest, Greeley looked at the rest of the photos. One youth athletic team after another. Quint was in photos with the teenagers. Other adults stood with teams of younger children.

"Does Damian Trucking sponsor these teams?" Greeley asked.

"Quint's idea. About six years ago, Jack and Quint were working late and a couple of neighborhood teenagers climbed the fence. You may have noticed this isn't the wealthiest of neighborhoods." She saw Greeley's nod. "I thought so."

Greeley knew the older woman meant because Greeley was Fern's daughter.

"Quint caught two of them. Said if they had so much free time, they could sweep his floors. Jack said before long the boys were telling Quint how their dads had abandoned their families. Quint knows about having no father, so he hired the boys to help around the place, and pretty soon he was gathering up boys and girls to play sports. He recruited some of our employees to help coach. Once Quint makes up his mind to do something, he's like a truck speeding downhill. Easier to ride him down than get out of the way."

"I believe that." Greeley felt the woman expected more from her. "I think it's great he sponsors some teams."

"Sponsors, funds, coaches. That's Quint, he sees a problem and he sets out to fix it."

Greeley walked slowly down the wall of pictures, then came to a dead halt in front of a photo of a man dressed as Santa Claus. "Is this Quint?"

"Our usual Santa got stuck in a blizzard on the western slope so Quint took over that year. He's big on Christmas. Instead of exchanging gifts at work, we have a food, clothing and toy drive for a local charity, and Quint provides a couple of trucks, drivers and helpers to load and unload Christmas baskets. To thank everyone, he throws a big holiday dinner at a local fancy restaurant."

Moving on to an enchanting picture of a small girl in a wheelchair with a huge yellow dog at her side, Greeley threw Mrs. Curtis an inquiring look.

"Quint went to the pound for a guard dog and came back with Barney and four other dogs and two cats. Found homes for all of them. Paid their licensing fees, for shots, all that. One of the drivers mentioned his daughter badly wanted a dog, but they didn't have a fenced yard, and his daughter is physically challenged. Quint organized a fence-raising party and found one of those dogs trained to fetch and carry.''

This unexpected side to Quint surprised and disturbed Greeley. It was easier to dislike a one-dimensional Quint. Hiding her reaction to the older woman's narrative, she said lightly, "He's quite the humanitarian, isn't he?"

The older woman pursed her lips before saying in an arctic voice, "Fern sneers at Quint's efforts, too. Says he's wasting his time." She bent over some papers, signaling an end to their conversation.

Suppressing a sigh, Greeley turned back to the photographs. Quint wore a grin as goofy as the teenagers in this picture. One youth held aloft a huge trophy.

She smiled at Quint as Santa Claus. His pillow had slipped, but he was clearly having the time of his life. She could almost hear his full belly laugh. He made a fabulous Santa.

He'd make a fabulous father.

Greeley shoved her hands in the back pockets of her jeans. Maybe he'd broken up with Fern because he considered her too old to bear his children.

He wanted children uncontaminated with Fern Kelly's blood.

Unless Fern had dumped baby girls over the entire state of Colorado, Quint Damian shouldn't have any trouble finding a wife who met his singular requirements.

Greeley sat back in Quint's chair and surveyed his home office. An enormous, heavy, wooden table with ornate carving dominated the room. The high shelf running around the perimeter of the room held an assortment of metal toy trucks which bore the rust and dents of heavy use. More old posters advertising Damian Trucking hung haphazardly on the walls. If Quint Damian had a hobby, he didn't advertise it.

The telephone on the table rang, then rang again. Should she answer it? What if it was a personal call for Quint? A girlfriend? It could be his grandfather or Fern calling about their plans. Greeley picked up the receiver. "Hello."

"Who is this?" a female voice asked.

"Greeley Lassiter."

"Lassiter?" A split second later the woman answered her own question in an extremely antagonistic voice. "Oh, Fern's daughter. Where's Quint?"

"He's swimming laps."

"Tell him the minute he climbs out of the pool he's to call his mother."

The phone slammed in Greeley's ear.

Another member of the club who obviously believed like birth mother, like daughter. Suddenly Greeley longed to talk to someone who didn't believe that. Picking up the phone, she dialed a familiar number.

"Yo," a deep male voice answered.

"Is that any way to answer a phone? Mom must not be home."

Worth laughed. "She's at Cheyenne's. About time you called. You and Fern busy doing the mother-daughter thing?"

Unwilling to debate the wisdom of staying in Denver while Fern was in Maui, Greeley muttered, "Not exactly," and hastily changed the subject. "Quint has commissioned me to do a sculpture as a gift for his grandfather."

"Has he?"

"The exposure will be good for me and should introduce me to the Denver art scene."

"Uh-huh."

"It's a great opportunity for me."

"Uh-huh."

"Cheyenne will be thrilled."

"Which has always been your mission in life, right?"

"You don't need to sound so skeptical. It's not like the commission's a ploy to persuade me to sabotage Fern's wedding to his grandfather."

"What Damian wants is to get you in his bed."

"That is the dumbest thing... Honestly, Worth, you think every man who so much as looks at one of your sisters wants to seduce her. I'm not a child. I can take care of myself and I don't hop into bed with every Tom, Dick and Harry who's interested." An ugly notion turned her stomach. "Maybe you think I do?"

"Nope. I think you're my baby sister and you've gone to Denver with a man who looks at you the same way Hannah looks at an ice cream cone."

"You couldn't be more wrong. I'm about as popular around here as a deer mouse spreading lethal hantavirus."

"Why? What'd you do?"

"If that isn't just like you, Worth Lassiter, assuming I'm to blame. The only thing I did was get born. Fern would like to forget I exist, and Quint looks at me and sees Fern."

"Come home. Let those people fight their own battles. You don't need Damian's commission. You're so talented, your star will soar without him."

"Thank you." Her brother's faith in her meant a lot.

"But you're not coming home," he said in a resigned voice.

"I told you. I'm thinking about trying to make the sculpture Quint says he wants." She could almost hear Worth's disapproval humming over the wires. "Don't act like my big brother. I'm not the least bit interested in Quint, and I have no intention of sleeping with him. He doesn't like me any better than I like him."

"That's what I'm afraid of," Worth said cryptically and hung up.

Greeley banged the receiver back in its cradle. A sound alerted her and she turned. Quint stood in the doorway.

CHAPTER SEVEN

QUINT WONDERED why Greeley found it necessary to lie to her half-brother. Her kisses weren't the kisses of a disinterested woman. She was interested in Quint, no matter how often she insisted otherwise.

And she was wrong about him. He was *very* interested in her. Quint didn't like it, but he didn't deny it. Propping a shoulder against the door jamb, he eyed her thoughtfully. "You seem to spend an inordinate amount of time denying you're interested in me."

Pink tinted her cheeks. "Who said I was talking about you?"

"You said my name. How many Quints do you know?"

"Okay, so I was talking about you." The admission obviously annoyed her, and she added quickly, "It's not my fault every single person on this planet thinks you're attracted to me. What am I supposed to do? Take out an ad in the newspaper telling everyone you're not?" she asked with a pugnacious look on her face.

The way she pointed her haughty little nose somewhere between him and the ceiling amused him. And made him want to toss her on his desk and see how long it took to turn haughty into something quite different. Under the circumstances, a preposterous—and dangerous—idea. His mouth twisted wryly. "Actually, the gods must have a perverse sense of humor, because I am attracted to you. I'd think you'd have figured that out by now." Her mouth dropped open. He gave her thirty seconds to come up with a response.

It took her five. "You don't even like me."

He went with the truth. "I don't have to *like* you to want to rip off your clothes."

Her eyes darkened with shock, and she picked up the telephone. "Don't you come near me or I'll dial 911."

As if he couldn't make it across the room before she'd finished dialing the nine. If he'd wanted to. He didn't. "I'm not going to attack you. Or seduce you."

"You couldn't seduce me."

He could.

And she could give lessons in how to infuriate a man. Instead of feeling grateful for his restraint, she had to challenge him. Quint couldn't decide if he wanted to kiss her or strangle her. Smothering both impulses, he leaned down and petted Barney. He was coming dangerously close to forgetting she was Fern's daughter. He reminded both of them. "I'm not interested in casual sex with unsuitable females."

Barney's tags jingled in the dead silence that met Quint's deliberately offensive remark. Paper rustled, then came the sound of pencils being gathered up. Quint heard the chair move back from his desk. He concentrated on scratching behind Barney's ears.

"I'm glad you feel that way," Greeley said in a cool, detached voice. "Unwanted admirers are such a bore."

He couldn't help looking up and asking, "Unwanted?"

She did her best, but disdain sat oddly on her face. "You're hardly my type."

So that's how she intended to play it. Deny everything. Pretend she wasn't interested. He gave her a long, narrow-eyed look. "From a purely academic standpoint, I'm curious, what is your type?" The triumphant gleam in her eyes told him he'd given the hoped-for response.

"Not what is, what isn't." She practically purred. "And what isn't, is a man who's so proud of his heroic, purebred pedigree he thinks he's better than anyone else."

Quint snapped upright, but she hadn't finished.

"I have news for you, Quint Damian. You are not the man who saved that platoon and went to prison camp, and you are not the man who died rescuing men from a burning plane.''

He turned to stone. When she swept past him, he couldn't have stopped her if he'd wanted to. He didn't. She'd spoken the truth. Quint wasn't one of those men.

He never would be.

Greeley stared at the darkened ceiling. Muted traffic sounds came through the screened window. Sounds far inferior to a cow mooing or horses calling to each other. City sounds were for people who belonged in the city.

She didn't belong here.

She was homesick. No wonder sleep wouldn't come.

She was rude.

Her ugly words echoed in her head in an unrelenting, painful refrain. What kind of monster mocked the undeniably heroic actions of a man's father and grandfather? Quint's father had died, and she'd thrown his death in Quint's face, lashing out at Quint in anger because he'd hurt her feelings.

She knew better.

When Greeley was eight, a schoolmate had called her a bastard. Greeley had reduced the girl to hysterical tears by yelling that the girl was so fat and ugly her own mother hated her. The horrified look on the girl's face before she burst into tears had given Greeley immense satisfaction—a satisfaction replaced in about two seconds by crushing guilt.

The guilt had mushroomed throughout the school day. Greeley had run straight from the school bus to her mother to confess what she'd done. Mary Lassiter had driven Greeley immediately to the girl's home to apologize and tell the child what she'd said wasn't true. Then Mary had shown Greeley where a long-ago cowboy had carved his initials in an old cottonwood tree. The raw wound had healed, but the scar remained.

The lesson had not been lost on Greeley. From that day on, she'd done her best to control her temper.

Until this evening.

It was all Quint Damian's fault—rejecting Greeley because of her birth.

No. The easy shifting of blame was a coward's way out. Quint hadn't put the ugly words in her mouth or forced her to say them.

A conscience was an uncomfortable companion. She had to apologize. If he interpreted her angry remarks and subsequent apology as signs she was interested in him, that was the price she had to pay for her contemptible behavior.

Knowing what she had to do and resolving to do it partially eased her conscience but did nothing to help her sleep.

At home, she'd have saddled up and gone for a ride. In the city, in an unfamiliar neighborhood, she didn't dare go jogging.

The lap pool.

Greeley jumped out of bed. A dark T-shirt and underpants would have to do surrogate duty as a swim suit. She didn't expect an audience, but one needed to honor rules of modesty.

Once the initial shock subsided, Greeley's body acclimated to the water's cool temperature, and she set a brisk pace, swimming from one end of the lap pool to the other and back again. When her muscles were reduced to the approximate firmness of jellyfish, she rolled onto her back, closed her eyes, and floated on the water's placid surface. Eventually she summoned the strength to pull herself from the water. Hastily toweling her exposed skin, she reached for the bottom of her sodden T-shirt to pull it off over her head.

"Reluctant though I am to do so, I suppose I ought to mention you're not alone."

The unexpected voice almost sent Greeley toppling back into the pool. She clutched the towel in front of her. "What are you doing in here? Spying on me?"

"Barney's fussing at the pool-room door woke me," Quint

said. "You'd think after all this time he'd have learned he's not going to get in here, but he never abandons hope."

"That doesn't answer why you're in here." Enough light entered the pool room's windows to reveal Quint sitting in a small wicker settee, his legs stretched out in front of him.

"Lifeguard duties. I didn't know how well you could swim. You should have mentioned you planned to use the pool."

"I can swim just fine. Which you should have figured out in about two minutes. You didn't need to stay."

"You swim a mean lap. I had the distinct feeling you weren't swimming for exercise so much as getting something—or someone—out of your system."

Turning her back to him, Greeley pulled on her robe over her wet clothing. There was no reason to wait until morning to apologize for her inexcusable remarks. She toweled her hair vigorously. So easy to make the remarks. So hard to take them back. Draping the towel over her shoulders, she combed her hair with her fingers. "I'm sorry about what I said," she mumbled to the floor. "Your grandfather and your father were very brave men and I had no right to belittle their heroic actions just because you annoyed me."

After a minute he said, "Nothing you say can take away from what they did. They'll always be heroes."

"Yes." Greeley drew on the cool tile floor with a wet toe. The silence lengthened awkwardly. She had to say something. "It's super what you do with the kids. The youth-league teams and all."

"Cheaper to fund a few teams than to deal with the aftermath of vandalism."

Snugging her robe with the belt, she faced him. "It's more than that. Your secretary said you coach."

The dark bulk shrugged. "Good exercise."

"Was playing Santa Claus good exercise, too?"

"Yeah, well..."

The thread of embarrassment running through his voice

told Greeley her praise disconcerted him. She curled into a wicker chair across the room from where he sat. Talking to him in the dark made conversation easier. She couldn't see his face. His eyes. His wide shoulders. "Would you answer something for me?"

A minute or two passed before he answered cautiously, "Maybe."

"If you didn't date Fern, and she didn't dump you, why do you dislike her so vehemently? It's one thing to dislike her because she's stealing part of your inheritance, but it's another to hate anyone even remotely connected with her."

"I don't hate you," he said swiftly.

The clammy T-shirt chilled her skin. "You don't know a thing about me, but you've repeatedly said you don't want to be involved with me because of Fern."

"Disappointed?"

His voice charged the simple question with a sexual heat, curling Greeley's damp toes and fluttering her insides. She shifted in the chair and adjusted her robe. He was trying to distract her. "I'm disappointed you won't tell me the truth."

"Being such a truthful person yourself."

"I tell the truth."

"Do you? Were you telling the truth when you denied any sexual attraction between us? When you said you weren't interested in me? When you said you didn't want to kiss me?" The disembodied voice from the small sofa baited Greeley.

She wanted to scream, "Yes!" She said nothing.

"That's what I thought." His voice oozed satisfaction. "And you lied when you claimed you didn't want to meet or know anything about your mother."

Greeley stirred. "She's not my mother."

He made an impatient sound. "You know what I mean."

"Yes." She cinched her robe tighter. "I didn't exactly lie," she said at last. "I thought it was true when I said it."

"You convinced yourself it was true."

"No. Maybe. All right." She hesitated. "If I tell you the truth, will you tell me the truth?"

"I won't lie, but I might not tell you everything."

Greeley considered his words. She had no intention of baring all her secrets either. In a way it would be a relief to talk to a faceless shadow. She couldn't disappoint Quint; he didn't care about her.

Her life had been spent trying not to disappoint the family who'd done so much for her.

"People use *bastard* as a casual curse these days. No one pays any attention to the word, unless one *is* a bastard. I had nothing to say about Beau and Fern messing around, nothing to say about who my father was or who my mother was, nothing to say about Fern abandoning me. Yet, I'm the bastard. A lucky bastard, someone once called me."

A muttered swear word came out of the darkness.

"It's true. Mom's been unbelievably good to me. And Worth and Cheyenne and Allie. They really do regard me as their real sister. They don't care who gave birth to me. They've never resented me. And they could have. Their father cheated on their mother. They had to share their mother's time and attention with someone who didn't belong."

"You're a Lassiter, the same as they are."

She made a face, forgetting he couldn't see her in the dark. "I didn't grow up on the 'Lassiter place.' I grew up on the 'Nichols place.' The ranch was started by Jacob and Anna Nichols, Mom's ancestors, not Beau's, not mine."

"Did your step-brother and step-sisters throw that in your face when you were growing up?"

"No. We fight and squabble like any other siblings, and they might call me thick-headed or stubborn or impossible, but they'd never call me an outsider. Or a bastard. They don't think my blood is contaminated."

Greeley, paused, waiting for him to apologize for implying that very thing. No apology came. Maybe her pathetic tale had put him to sleep.

Mildly irritated, she continued, "Fern gave birth to me. I had nothing to say about it, and nothing anyone does can ever change that. What if someone told you you were totally unsuitable because you have your mother's green eyes?"

A sudden recollection hit her. "Oh my gosh, a woman called, your mother, I think, and she said you were to call her the instant you finished swimming. I totally forgot, because, well..." Because she'd been too busy saying nasty things. "She'll be positive I deliberately didn't tell you."

"Why would Mom think that?" He'd been silent so long, the sound of his voice came almost as a surprise.

"She turned absolutely hostile when I identified myself. What did Fern do to you people?"

Quint exhaled loudly. "Maybe I do owe you that much." Not rushing to explain, he eventually said, "Granddad's wife, my grandmother, died in childbirth, along with her baby. My dad was just a young boy, but they took him to the hospital to see her. I guess they knew she was dying. She made my dad promise to take care of his father. Their first baby had died, and grief had nearly sent Granddad over the edge. My father took his promise seriously, and when he went off to war, he made Mom promise she'd take care of Granddad if he didn't come home."

"So she moved you and her in here." Until she'd remarried. "How old were you when your mom married again?"

"Nineteen."

Old enough to take care of his grandfather. "Your mother asked you to take over her promise so she could remarry," Greeley said slowly, the picture coming together for her.

"Mom turned Phil down when he first asked her. It took Phil and I months to convince her I was perfectly capable of watching out for Granddad."

Greeley had the last piece of the puzzle. "And you resent Fern, an outsider, encroaching on your promise."

"You can't seriously believe marrying Fern is in Granddad's best interests? You, of all people, ought to know Fern's primary interest in life is Fern. She doesn't care about Granddad, she cares about his money and the kind of life he can give her.''

"If the arrangement makes him happy, what difference does it make why she's marrying him?''

"Marriage isn't an arrangement. It's selfless love and devotion. It's worrying on your deathbed about the one you love. It's committing your life to raising a grandson. It's keeping a promise to your dying mother, keeping a promise to the man who loved you.''

"Your grandmother had no business placing that kind of burden on a child. And your dad—he went to the Air Force Academy and then learned to be a pilot, knowing he could be sent off to war someday. He probably married your mother so he'd have someone to shift his burden to. He got it off his conscience and onto hers.

"And if your mom was so self-sacrificing, why'd she ask you to shoulder the burden as soon as you were old enough? A sensible person would have told you the promise was stupid and ridiculous instead of making it into some kind of precious family legacy. I thought your grandfather was an adult, and an adult doesn't need you or anyone else sacrificing his life for him. Your family doesn't know about loving, they know about using.''

"I should have known you wouldn't understand,'' he said coldly.

She couldn't quit now. "Because you think I inherited Fern's irresponsible and selfish nature. You're wrong. What I know about families I learned from my mother. My real mother. Mary Lassiter. She gave us the tools to stand on our own two feet and expected us to do so. She didn't treat us like frail ninnies and make us weak. Love makes a person strong. Your grandfather is a classic example of the tyranny of the weak.''

"You know nothing about my grandfather.''

"I know he started a successful business that thrives today.

He's not my idea of a weakling who needs to be mollycoddled." The truth hit her. "He knows all about the family promise. Knows and uses it. What better way to keep his family attached to him, dancing to his tunes?"

"I don't know where you picked up this ludicrous babble, but you have no idea what you're talking about."

Greeley ignored his disparaging remark. "He's been using you and your mother for years," she said slowly, "only now he's met Fern and you're no longer enough for him. He wants a wife who's attractive and younger than him, but the family promise won't work to tie Fern to him, so he's dangling his business in front of her. Shoving you aside."

"I'm not being shoved aside."

"You are." Things became clearer. "I knew you were hiding something. I couldn't put my finger on it, but I see it now."

"I'm sure you're dying to share your grand vision."

A dangerous note in his quiet voice raised the hair on Greeley's neck. Only a fool disturbed a sleeping bear. She debated backing off. Running for cover. Hiding her true thoughts and feelings. An exercise she excelled at.

"Lose your nerve?"

The taunting question decided her. She couldn't accuse his grandfather of weakness and then surrender to her own weaknesses. Taking a deep breath, she said, "It doesn't take nerve to point out a truth you already know. You think you're being shoved aside for Fern and that's why you're so bitter toward her. She'd be taking your grandfather and the business away from you. No wonder you're furious. Your father abandoned you, your mother abandoned you and now your grandfather plans to abandon you."

He made an odd sound. "That is the most asinine thing you've said yet."

Quint slumped against the back of the settee, relief driving the stiffness from his body. She didn't know. She didn't have a clue. He wanted to laugh out loud at the nonsense she uttered with such certainty.

"It's not asinine," she said. "I'm not condemning you for your feelings, but if your grandfather is as wonderful as you claim, he'll always love you, no matter who he marries. So what if he leaves all or part of the business to Fern? You're young. Start your own business. Your grandfather did. You're not dependent on him. You could do anything."

Her earnest, encouraging voice reminded him of his mother telling him he could do anything he wanted when he grew up. Quint suspected Greeley would be a great mother, giving her child the security of knowing he was deeply loved.

He visualized her breast-feeding a child. Rocking him to sleep. Being there for her child. Always.

Quint blinked away the images. Greeley's qualifications for motherhood had nothing to do with him. In fact, he pitied whoever married her. The poor sap would never know what went on behind her innumerable disguises.

She hadn't finished. "I know all about being abandoned, and I understand how it affects a person's life. I always expect people to abandon me. It's hard to be trusting with our kind of background, but honestly, Quint, if your grandfather loves you, he'll never abandon you."

Unexpected sympathy welled up inside him. Poor little, brave, abandoned baby. She was reassuring him. He thought about that. Maybe she was reassuring herself. He wanted to take her in his arms, and kiss away the pain of her past.

It occurred to him she'd given him a precious gift. Not the pep talk. The way she'd stepped from behind a mask to reveal a part of herself. For a mistress of disguise, allowing him a glimpse of her inner self must be terrifying. The strained, self-conscious way she spoke told him of the courage it took for her to admit to her fears.

Quint's fingers tightened on the braided arms of the wicker furniture. He possessed no such courage.

He had to say something before she misinterpreted his silence. Before she fled back to her hiding place. "I appreciate your concern," he said carefully, "but the situation isn't about Granddad abandoning me. It's about my failure to protect him. I'm the one who hired Fern. And then I mishandled the situation that arose. I should have anticipated her intentions and fired her before she dug her claws into him."

"Did you ever consider perhaps she loves him?"

"No. I was her first choice for a ticket to easy street, and that's not my inflated ego talking. When Fern realized she couldn't have me, she went after Big Ed with a vengeance. To prove she could. To spite me." He made a fist and smacked the arm of the settee. "She'll destroy him," he said flatly.

"By my count, he's lost three children and his wife and he's survived. What can Fern do to him?"

"I don't care if he marries or if he has lady friends throughout Colorado. As long as he's happy. I wouldn't care if he married Fern if she'd make him happy. She won't."

"You don't know that. Maybe she loves him." Her words lacked conviction.

"Loves him," he repeated contemptuously. "Fern is selfish, grasping, self-involved and totally incapable of loving anyone but herself. She's made a career out of dumping people the second they become inconvenient or superfluous. When she's through with Granddad she'll walk away without a backward glance at the wreckage she's leaving behind." Greeley's defense of her mother riled him. "You ought to know all about being dumped by Fern."

Quint winced as his last words reverberated in the dark room. Only a jerk rubbed her nose in it. "Sorry," he said in a clipped voice.

"Don't worry about it," she said brightly.

Too brightly. He'd driven her back into hiding. He hated emotional women. She'd had over twenty years to face the reality of what kind of woman her mother was. She had no right to make him feel guilty. "I'm sorry," he repeated stiffly, "I didn't mean to upset you, but you're the one who said you didn't want to be treated like a frail ninny. I thought you were strong enough to face the truth."

"You're absolutely right." She stood. "You didn't upset me. Good night."

Her chipper voice didn't fool him for a second. He had a vision of her weeping into her pillow. Guilt ripped at his guts. He couldn't let her go off to bed like this. As she neared, light from a three-quarter moon shone on her face. Her uplifted chin. Her mouth, so determinedly resolute.

He didn't buy any of it. Quint touched her arm. "Don't go yet. Sit and talk to me some more."

Greeley didn't walk away. Or join him on the settee. She stood as immobile as the sculptures she created.

"You spent the day checking out every facet of our operation," Quint said. "Anything inspire you? Get any ideas for Granddad's sculpture?"

She turned her head. A passing cloud hid the moon, shadowing her face. "No." Her cool voice dared him to make something of her answer.

"You will."

"Why will I? Because you say so?"

"Because it interests you. You stuck that pointy nose everywhere. I'd be seriously amazed if any work got done in the shop. You impressed the mechanics." First with her tight jeans, then with her knowledge. "More than one told me you weren't just a pretty face. That's pretty high praise."

Genuine pleasure rippled through her answering laughter. For once she wasn't faking or hiding how she felt. Quint felt a curious urge to know more about the real Greeley. The one she normally kept hidden behind her various masks. He tugged her toward the settee.

She settled comfortably beside him. "One of your mechanics said I'm the first woman who didn't say something about how big truck tires are. I've always wondered what one of those sleeper cabs looked like on the inside. Davy's going to be green with envy."

Quint stretched his arm along the back of the settee. He had to put it somewhere. "You have quite a family."

"You mean because Mom didn't give birth to me, and Cheyenne didn't give birth to Davy, and Allie didn't give birth to Hannah, we're some kind of kooky, oddball bunch."

"No, I meant it's nice the way you all stick together."

"Grandpa Yancy wouldn't have agreed with you," she said, her voice warm with amusement. "He thought we stuck together too much, that we got in trouble because there were three of us, and we knew Worth would rescue us."

"What kind of trouble can three girls get in?"

"It depends. If Cheyenne started it, it was because she'd stuck her nose where it didn't belong. When Cheyenne sees an injustice she wades right in, and she expected Allie and I to be right behind her."

"And Allie? Never mind. I can guess. Abused animals."

She nodded, her hair gleaming in the pale moonlight.

Quint lifted a damp strand and tugged gently. "And you?" At first he didn't think she was going to answer.

"I got in fights and ran away."

Her defiant voice warned him to tread carefully. "Did Allie and Cheyenne run away with you?" He watched her pick at her robe, then smooth it over her knees.

"They came after me. With Worth."

"What about the fighting? I'll bet your half-sisters have wicked right-hand punches."

"They've always been tall. Just standing behind me usually was enough to scare anyone off."

"They don't look that mean to me." He felt her shrug.

"Well, we never talked about it, but a couple of the bigger boys who teased me showed up later with black eyes or swollen noses."

"And you think Allie and Cheyenne took them out behind the barn and taught them a few manners?"

"No, I think Worth found out what happened. Because of Beau, Worth always said we had to take care of Mom and each other. Lassiters stick together."

"Sound like some kind of precious family legacy to me." Quint slid his fingers down another strand of hair.

She inhaled sharply. "I suppose you might think that, but it's different than with your family. It's not a burden for us, we do it because we love each other."

He played with her hair, not bothering to answer. Waiting for her to realize how illogical her words sounded. She didn't disappoint him.

"I guess it's different when it's your own family," she said lamely. "Worth claims I'm the most judgmental, which makes no sense at all because I should be the least judgmental."

"Granddad likes to say that the best defense is a good offense." He wound damp hair around a finger. "Attack before you get attacked."

She sighed. "Allie says I'm a porcupine."

Chemical odors from the lap pool rose in the humid air to mingle with the smell of damp earth from the potted plants. A landscape service took care of the gardening inside and out, so Quint had no idea which plant gave off the heavy perfume that tickled his senses.

Wicker creaked as Greeley shifted position. A faint smell of chlorine clung to her hair. Her skin. Her robe covered her from head to toe, but not for one second did he forget she wore nothing underneath it but a wet T-shirt. He wondered if she was as aware as he was of her thigh touching his. "I've seen porcupines. Fat little suckers that waddle along."

"That's not what she meant," Greeley said indignantly. "She was talking about the way they get all bristly the minute they're..." Her voice trailed off.

"Scared?"

"Whatever."

He wondered if she ever admitted her fears to anyone.

Quint knew about being scared. About wondering if you'd be left alone to fend for yourself. Wondering if you'd ever measure up. His fingers tightened around her hair. "Your hair's wet."

She turned her face up to his. Her teeth gleamed in the pale light. "Would you believe it? There's water in your pool."

Naturally he kissed her.

After making a tiny startled sound, she leaned into him, her lips soft and cool beneath his. "You taste like chlorine-flavored toothpaste," he said. He'd swear he heard a tiny giggle.

"Again, there's water in the pool."

He nibbled along her generous bottom lip. "When I saw you, I thought a mermaid had fallen from the sky."

"I think that's a terrible mix of metaphors or something," she said breathlessly, her head back against his shoulder, her throat tempting him.

He was in no mood to deny temptation.

"I didn't realize chlorine could taste so sexy," he muttered. She gave a little laugh, her throat muscles quivering against his lips.

Quint worked his way up the side of her neck until he gently captured her smooth earlobe between his teeth.

She tugged her ear free. "I hate that. It always gives me the creeps."

Sudden, irrational jealousy hit him. "Be sure and tell me what other men do that you do like," he said coldly.

She went very still. "I've been kissed before. Did you think I've lived my life in a convent? I assume I'm not the first woman you've kissed." Her hands lay clasped in her lap.

Quint picked one up. A sturdy, callused hand which belied her delicate face. One by one he kissed the short, sturdy fingers. Artistic fingers. He didn't buy into the myth that an artist needed long, elegant fingers. "You're the first artist I've kissed."

Her tension eased. "You're the first boss of a trucking company I've kissed."

"How many truck drivers have you kissed?" He started on the other hand.

"I don't think I've ever kissed a truck driver." She spoke in fits and starts, her words punctuated by shallow breaths.

"There you go. Another first."

"You can actually drive those trucks?"

The awed admiration in her voice brought a halt to his kissing. He gave a low laugh. "You mean I've been pretending I have etchings to show women in order to tempt them into my clutches, and what really turns them on is that I have my commercial driver's license and can drive a big truck?"

"You didn't say anything about any etchings to me," she said demurely.

His body tightened. His male hormones went into overdrive. Slow down, he told himself. Greeley lightly traced his jawbone with her finger. He felt as if he were in a truck speeding down a steep hill. His brain screamed at him to apply the brakes.

The darkness concealed the color of her eyes. Would they be bluer or grayer when she made love?

A warning light went on in his head. She was a mistress of a million disguises. Since he'd met her, she'd worn so many layers of masks, she'd made his head spin.

His head was spinning now.

Quint wanted to strip every mask from her. He didn't care that she was Fern Kelly's daughter. He wanted to make love to her.

"Suppose I said I had some etchings in my bedroom," he said slowly. "Would that interest you?"

If she said yes, he'd forget who she was and take her to his bed.

CHAPTER EIGHT

HIS QUESTION terrified her, because she was interested. She knew Quint wasn't talking about etchings. He was inviting her to share his bed. Greeley snatched her hand from his face and buried it in her lap with her other hand, before she slid them over his bare shoulders. When Worth walked barefoot around the house wearing nothing but sweatpants, her pulse didn't race or her face warm. She laced her fingers tightly together.

Quint's leg touched hers, burning her through two layers of fabric. What had she been thinking, kissing him again? The first time she'd used a welding torch, the man who showed her how it worked had warned her repeatedly about the danger of playing with fire. "It wouldn't be a good idea."

He combed his fingers through her hair. "I've had nothing but bad ideas from the second I agreed to go to Aspen looking for you."

His words hurt. Even so, the feel of his fingers against her scalp might have tempted her. If she was braver. If she were someone else. If he wasn't a man who couldn't forgive her for being related to Fern Kelly. "Well, that's that then, isn't it?"

"You don't think it's a good idea either," he said, almost defensively, as if she'd goaded him into the response.

"Of course I don't." So why was she tempted? "We're totally wrong for each other. There's no future in us sleeping together."

He didn't need to belabor the point. "I agree. If I can't stop Granddad marrying Fern, we're bound to resent each other. Me, because you're her daughter no much how you deny it. And you, because you know how I feel about her."

131

"I'm not arguing with you." She wished he'd quit playing with her hair.

"No matter what happens, you'll resent me wanting to use you to break them up. You'd think I slept with you to manipulate you." His fingers tightened in her hair.

"Would that be why?"

"No." He lowered his head. "This would be why," he muttered against her mouth.

She explored his chest and shoulders with the tips of her fingers. He was hard bone, tough sinew, and warm, smooth skin. Tiny bumps that responded to her explorations.

As she responded to his kisses, his caresses, her breasts swelled, the hard tips pressing against her cold, clammy T-shirt. Then his hands covered them, warming, no, heating them. Greeley leaned into him.

Quint lifted his head. "Get out of here," he said, an angry, guttural edge to his voice, "before I forget you're a guest in my house."

Greeley fled. A loud splash sounded behind her. She closed the door without turning around.

The water was too warm. He needed polar seas. Quint resolutely stroked the length of the pool. He lost count of the laps he swam. Lost count of the times he asked himself, why not? One night. She'd been willing. No matter what she said. He could have persuaded her. All he'd wanted was to sleep with her. Simple enough. It wasn't as if he was proposing marriage.

That thought went a long way toward cooling him off.

Greeley might not be much like her mother, but he refused to have Fern Kelly for a mother-in-law. A smart man would marry an orphan. The last thing he needed was more family making demands on him, raising expectations he couldn't hope to meet.

As for Greeley, she needed a strong man. One who looked past her aggressive facade and saw the needy child. A man would want to spend his life assuring her he'd be there for her. Be her hero.

He wasn't anybody's idea of a hero.

The significance of clicking doggy toenails didn't hit Quint until he looked up and saw Barney launch himself at the pool. The dog hit with a joyous splash and paddled joyfully toward Quint. Laughing, Quint treaded water. "Sure, you're happy now, but what about when you decide you want out, you fat, little, short-legged sausage?" Catching the dog, Quint made his way to the side of the pool and heaved Barney onto the tile floor. "Sit. Stay." He should have added, "Don't shake."

Placing his hands on the pool deck, Quint started to lever himself out of the pool. At the last second he saw Fern sitting in the settee he'd abandoned. "You've come back."

"Obviously. The dog got in before I could stop him." She'd never been crazy about Barney.

Quint eased back into the pool. "Where's Granddad?"

"Carrying in the luggage." Her voice changed, lowered seductively. "Aren't you going to jump out of the pool and give me a welcome-home hug?" She mockingly waved his sweatpants in the air.

"I'm not through with my swim."

"I'll wait." Fern made a show of settling back. "Have you and the girl been having fun? Has she been boring you with childish confidences?"

Quint didn't think Fern would be pleased to hear he could hardly keep his hands off her anything-but-boring daughter. He shrugged. "She babbles. I don't have to listen."

Fern gave an unladylike snort. "I'll bet you listen hard enough when she's talking about how her mother 'done her wrong.'"

"What makes you think she does?"

"You kidding? After being raised by that puritanical martyr, Mary Lassiter? Beau thought she walked on water. He was always talking about Mary this and Mary that. I had her up to here." She gestured at her neck. "If someone had dumped a kid on me, I'd have dumped the kid right back, but that woman took her like I'd handed her the newspaper. Then her and her oldest kid looked at me like I was cow—" She abruptly stopped.

Quint let the silence ride, interested that after all these years, Fern's resentment of Mary Lassiter rankled enough to disturb the polished veneer Fern exhibited to the world. Too bad Granddad hadn't been present to hear her diatribe. Barney shook again, spraying water and jingling his dog tags.

"You stupid dog," Fern said in irritation, "you're getting me all wet." Her voice turned flirtatious as she addressed Quint. "You're going to turn into a prune."

"I'm fine."

"Edward worried about you and her alone in the house here. I told him you'd be a gentleman. I knew she'd be safe. You'd never condescend to being interested in my illegitimate brat. Quinton Damian is much too good for the likes of me or my kin. What'll it take? A virgin debutante? A millionaire's daughter? Or both, to be eligible for the honored role of your wife?"

Big Ed striding through the door spared Quint the need to answer.

"There you two are. Honey, did you tell Quint about our trip? Why's Barney in here? How are things at the terminal? Where's Fern's daughter?"

"I assume Greeley's sleeping. As for Barney—"

"Quint must not have closed the door tight when he came in to swim," Fern said quickly. "I walked into the kitchen just in time to see the dog disappear through the door. I didn't know Quint was in here, so I rushed in to make sure the dog was okay."

Big Ed affectionately fondled Barney's ears. "You sneaky little son of a gun. You need to watch that door, Quint."

Fern stood. "I'm going to bed." She left the pool room.

"Too bad her little girl isn't up. Fern's dying to give her

the fancy dress she bought her." Big Ed herded Barney out of the room, then turned to look at Quint. "When there's women in the house, you shouldn't swim buck naked."

Quint lay back and floated, watching the moon move across the sky. Big Ed might be seventy-six, but he was still sharp as a tack.

Except when it came to Fern.

Quint wondered which Greeley would mention first, the dress or Fern. He doubted she'd refer to what had happened in the pool room.

She spoke the second they'd turned the corner at the end of the block. "That is the yellowest dress I've ever seen. I'll look as if I have terminal jaundice. I thought you'd burst a blood vessel trying not to laugh when you saw it."

Either she knew nothing about reading a man's face, or he'd disguised his gut reaction to her modeling the dress better than he'd thought. Seeing her in the dress, he'd immediately fantasized about placing her on his bed, the dress billowing around her as he slowly unbuttoned the thirty million buttons while she begged him to hurry. His imagination had painted the dress red. "You look better in red."

"I look better in every other color in the world than in that yellow. Fern couldn't have found a more inappropriate dress for me if she'd spend ten years looking. Have you ever seen so many ruffles? All I need is lacy white stockings and black patent-leather strap shoes and I'll look like Hannah."

Quint dragged his mind out of his bedroom. "There's your answer. The last thing Fern wants at her wedding is a gorgeous adult daughter."

She wasn't listening. "I wonder if I can get Barney to eat it or something. Your grandfather couldn't stop talking about how hard she shopped to find that dress. I'm afraid it'll hurt his feelings if I don't come up with a really good excuse for not wearing it."

Quint suspected she was right. Granddad realized he'd

goofed in forcing a meeting on Fern and Greeley, and he was determined to make them both happy—and mitigate his guilt.

Fern had worn a new pair of diamond stud earrings and a new bracelet consisting of a single strand of diamonds to breakfast. She seldom appeared at the breakfast table, and Big Ed obviously believed she'd made an effort on her daughter's behalf. Quint assumed she'd joined them to show off her new jewelry, another gift from Big Ed.

He glanced over at Greeley. She sat with bent head, picking at the ends of her fingers. Breakfast had been awkward. The manners his mother had taught him hadn't covered such a situation. Quint had eaten quickly, excused himself and tried to pry his grandfather from the table, but a crowbar couldn't have done that. Big Ed wanted to get to know Fern's daughter.

"Other than the dress, you okay?" Quint asked Greeley.

Her head snapped up. "I didn't spend the night writhing with unfulfilled desire, if that's what you mean," she said in a snippy voice.

He was glad one of them hadn't. He cleared his throat. "I meant breakfast this morning. Your first real meeting with your mother, and it wasn't exactly private."

Her face turned a cute, sexy shade of pink. "I knew what you meant. I was teasing."

A gentleman would let it go. "So you didn't writhe?"

"I fell asleep the second my head hit the pillow. I didn't even dream. How about you?"

He barely managed to swallow his irritation. She could have lied. "I writhed," he said grimly.

Stark silence met his admission, then Greeley reached over and turned on the radio. "I love this program. Hope you don't mind."

The morning traffic report blared from his car stereo speakers.

For a second she'd almost believed him, then common sense took hold. Men writhed over gorgeous blondes like Cheyenne and Allie. They didn't writhe over little brown sparrows, Greeley reminded herself that afternoon as she walked into the house from the garage. Quint stayed outside to talk to his grandfather and the man from the yard service.

"Who's there?" Fern called from the living room. "Oh," she said when she saw Greeley in the doorway, "it's you."

Greeley ignored the lukewarm reception, her attention caught by the mound of luggage sitting by the front door. "Going somewhere?"

"California. I got a job offer out there I couldn't refuse. Personal assistant to a movie producer, working for one of Hollywood's movers and shakers."

"But your wedding's less than two weeks away."

"Calling it off," Fern said briskly. "Edward's seventy-six. I don't want to spend what few good years I have left nursing an old man." She adjusted her diamond bracelet. "I'm leaving him a note. He'll understand. A man like Edward gets where he got by looking out for number one," she added callously.

"You're dumping him." Greeley clutched the back of the nearest chair in shock. "Just like you dumped me."

Fern gave her a belligerent look. "Don't you judge me. I was the oldest of nine kids. My dad took off for parts unknown and my mom waited tables, leaving me to take care of the brats. I left the day after I graduated from high school, and I swore I'd never be like my mother, having one kid after another. I learned from you. Never made that kind of mistake again."

"Nice to know I was your only mistake," Greeley said in a feeble attempt at sarcasm.

"Don't bother trying to make me feel guilty. I gave you a family and a home. Your dad swore she'd take you in and raise you proper." Fern made a face. "I know what I am. You don't like me, but I can look in the mirror."

A car horn honked outside.

"Do you need help with your luggage?" Funny how manners got you through even the most stupefying moments.

"The driver can get it. He might as well do something for his tip." Fern opened the door and signaled, then turned back to Greeley, nodding at a small white envelope on a side table. "See that Edward gets that." She waited for the taxi driver to collect her luggage, then picked up the two small remaining pieces. "I'd promise to keep in touch, but I'd be lying." She hesitated. "I don't see any point in us falling on each other's necks, so...good luck."

"Thank you." Greeley couldn't think of anything else to say. It didn't matter. She spoke to a fast-closing door.

Anger replaced her stunned disbelief. Fern Kelly had done it again. Gone her selfish way, not caring how much wreckage and debris she left in her wake. Did that kind of single-minded selfishness run in one's blood?

Greeley refused to believe that. She couldn't. Not when Fern's blood ran in her veins.

Fern's blood, but Mary Lassiter's code of conduct.

Gratitude and love for Mary cooled Greeley's anger. She almost pitied the woman who'd given birth to her. Fern would never know the joy and love and laughter that were commonplace around Mary's table.

Her mother loved her family, her son and daughters and sons-in-law and grandchildren. Mary would welcome Cheyenne's new baby into her heart as joyfully as she'd welcomed Davy and Hannah. And Greeley.

Intentionally or not, the woman who couldn't love had given Greeley to a woman who could.

Greeley walked numbly around the overstuffed chair and fell into it. She'd never see Fern Kelly again. With a few brutal words Fern had walked out of Greeley's life. Again.

Greeley didn't care.

She wanted to shout it to the rooftops. She didn't care. She had a mother who loved her, a family she belonged to. Fern Kelly didn't matter. Fern had never mattered.

"She gone yet?"

Greeley spun around. Edward Damian stood in the kitchen doorway. He had the saddest eyes she'd ever seen. "You know?"

"I was working in the yard and came in for a glass of water and heard her calling for a taxicab." His gaze went to the envelope. "I suppose she left a note."

Greeley nodded. Sympathy lumped in her throat as Quint's grandfather seemed to shrink before her eyes.

Quint chased Barney into the living room, laughing at the excited dog. At the sight of his grandfather's face, Quint stopped abruptly, his laughter hollow echoes in the room. "What's wrong?" he asked sharply.

When Edward didn't answer, Greeley said, "Fern's gone. She took a job in California."

Edward slowly nodded his head. "I thought it might be something like that." His shoulders hunched, he walked across the room.

Quint watched his grandfather with a deep frown on his face. "Are you okay, Granddad?"

"Fine. For an old fool." Edward picked up Fern's note with trembling fingers. "Expensive presents can't change me being more than thirty years older than her. I knew it couldn't last. I'm grateful for the time we did have together." He looked at Greeley. "I apologize for taking advantage of your mother before we married."

It took a second before Greeley realized he was referring to sleeping with Fern.

"Even though I committed to her in word and in my heart, I was wrong not to wait. I guess I hoped she wouldn't leave if we'd shared a bed." He gave a long sigh. "I'm going to lie down. I spent too long working in the yard today. I think I'll skip dinner. I'm not very hungry. There's a casserole in the refrigerator." Edward left the room, shuffling his feet as if he were a hundred years old.

Quint didn't explode until he'd followed Greeley into the

kitchen. Then he proceeded to call Fern every name Greeley had ever heard and a few that were totally new to her.

Keeping out of his way, Greeley read the housekeeper's instructions and put the casserole the woman had prepared in the oven for Quint's dinner. It would take her only a few minutes to pack and be on the road.

Quint kicked a kitchen chair and swore at the refrigerator.

"You got what you wanted," Greeley said. "Why aren't you celebrating?"

He gave her a killing glare. "I knew she'd hurt him. I wanted her out of his life before she had a chance to do her dirty work. I thought with you here, if she treated you the way she was sure to, Granddad would see her true character and know he didn't want her in his life."

His indifference to possible suffering on Greeley's part irritated her. "I hope you won't lose any sleep over my birth mother rejecting me again," she said in a saccharine voice.

"I won't. You had ample evidence of how she'd behave before you drove up here." He gave Greeley a look of dawning comprehension. "Don't blame me because she acted true to her character." He thrust his fingers through his hair. "Leopards don't change their spots."

"I know that, and I certainly wouldn't want you worrying that I'll be traumatized the rest of my life by this latest rejection."

"Don't start with me. It doesn't come as any surprise to you that she didn't want you here. You came because you wanted to ruin her fun." Quint kicked another chair. "This is all my fault." He banged his fist on the counter top. "I ought to be shot for hiring her." Walking over to a kitchen window, he stood with his back to Greeley, "Did you notice the way he literally aged before our eyes? He never naps."

Giving up trying to force sympathy from Quint, Greeley said with a confidence she didn't feel, "I'm sure he'll be fine."

Quint turned his head and glowered at her. "He won't be

fine," he ground out between his teeth. "Granddad's from the old school. He'll never forgive himself for having sex with her. She's probably already forgotten," Quint added bitterly. Facing the window again, he jammed his hands in his back pockets. Tension radiated from his set shoulders. "What do I do now?"

Greeley had no answers. In moments of crisis Mary Lassiter baked chocolate cakes. "Maybe you can persuade him to eat when the casserole is done. I set the timer for you."

There really wasn't anything she could do to help. Except leave. Her presence would only remind Edward—and Quint—of Fern. "It won't take me long to pack," she assured Quint's back.

He swung around, his forehead furrowed in a deep frown. "Where do you think you're going?"

"Home. The wedding's off. You don't need me here any longer."

"You can't leave."

"If you're worried about the sculpture, I'm sure I have enough notes and sketches."

"Forget about the sculpture. I'm talking about a man's life here, not some stupid pile of junk."

Greeley felt as if she'd been kicked in the stomach by a horse. Gradually, sounds filtered through her shock. Quint's harsh breathing. The ticking of the clock on the wall. Barney drinking water from his dog bowl in the utility room.

Pulling herself together, she carefully said, "I see." She could hardly avoid seeing. The sculpture, Quint's kisses, his pretense of being physically attracted to her. All lies. His rejection hurt infinitely more than Fern's had.

He was rejecting her professionally, Greeley told herself, not believing it for a minute. The truth was—no, she couldn't deal with the truth. Not now. Not yet. "I'm as big a fool as your grandfather, aren't I?" The question was rhetorical. She knew the answer.

Quint beat her to the doorway and barred her way with an

outstretched arm. "Don't be an idiot. I want the sculpture. It's just not the main thing on my mind right now." He yanked loose his tie. "You saw him. He's a broken man. I messed up everything." He looked over Greeley's head. "Granddad says my father always knew what to do. I really screwed up. You have to help me."

Greeley could scarcely believe her ears. "You drag me to Denver to use me, kiss me to make me pliable, lie to make me like you, call my sculptures junk and then ask me for help?"

He rubbed the back of his neck. "Just let it go, Greeley. We can fight later. Right now—" He stopped abruptly and gave her an arrested look. After a minute, he said, "Define *pliable*." Sexual awareness simmered in the back of his eyes.

She wanted to shoot him. "I meant stupid." *Stupid* definitely defined her behavior. Greeley took a deep breath. A big mistake. His scent filled her nostrils. Weakened her brain.

"My kisses make you stupid?" Lazy male satisfaction threaded through his voice.

She clamped her back teeth together until she thought she could speak without screaming. "I don't care to debate the innumerable causes of my stupidity. It's enough to know I'm stupid. But I'm not stupid enough to stay here." He could not use her words against her. His kisses weren't that potent.

If she lied to herself, that was his fault, too.

"I can't believe you're picking now to admit you like kissing me," Quint practically shouted at her. "What kind of lousy timing is that?"

She'd shoot him twice. Did he think she went around kissing every idiot who owned a sports car?

"Greeley…" Reaching over, he smoothed a hand over her hair. "I can't get distracted now. Not even by you. I have to save Granddad. Don't look at me like that."

"I'm not looking at you like anything."

"I never liked eyes the color of yours before. Thought they

were dull. I don't even know what color they are. A mish-mash of blue and gray.''

She would not listen. He was trying to manipulate her again. She'd given him the weapon. Used the word *pliable*.

"Sometimes your eyes are closed doors. Other times, like now, they're windows into your soul. I can read every thought that flits through your head.'' He smiled. A sexy, edgy, masculine smile. "You want to kiss me.''

"You're crazy,'' she managed to say.

She loved his mouth. Loved the way he kissed slow and deep. Loved the way she fit against his body. Loved how alive he made her feel. How special. She felt comforted. Whole. As if she'd come home.

Quint couldn't believe how good she felt in his arms. How right. She practically hummed under his kiss like a finely tuned engine. He felt her heat, her power. Breathing her scent, he thought of wildflowers. Quint lifted his head and cradled her face between his palms. "I must be crazy.'' Emotions shifted and tumbled in her eyes. The beautiful, indescribable color would haunt his dreams. "You know I want you.''

"Yes.'' Her eyes darkened. Sadness spilled out the corners. "There's not much logic to physical attraction, is there?'' She tried to smile. "Luckily, I don't think it's life-threatening.''

"You think that's all it is? Lust?''

"We don't even know each other.''

Quint had lusted after women before. He'd never before felt this overwhelming need to comfort and protect a woman. To keep her safe. To be her hero. The way his father had been his mother's hero. He couldn't be, of course. "I'm not perfect,'' he said out loud.

Sudden amusement danced in her eyes. "I may have only met you a few days ago, but I've figured that out. You're too single-minded to be perfect.'' Her teasing, under-the-eyelashes look took the sting out of her words.

And sent heat straight to his gut. Quint ran his hands loosely down her arms. ''Just think what you could learn about me if you stayed a little longer.''

Her eyes narrowed suspiciously. ''Entirely too single-minded.''

He would have kissed her again, but a sound came from the other end of the kitchen. His grandfather appeared in the doorway from the living room. His shoulders slumped, his facial muscles sagging, Big Ed was the picture of defeat. Quint stepped away from Greeley and tried for a light touch. ''Smelled dinner cooking and got hungry, huh?''

His grandfather shook his head. ''I couldn't sleep for thinking. Your mom and Phil are flying up in a few days.''

''I'll call them,'' Quint said.

''And the wedding. Things have to be canceled. People told.''

Quint didn't like his grandfather's lifeless voice. ''I'll take care of everything. Don't worry about it.''

Big Ed gestured helplessly. ''Fern made the arrangements. I'm not sure what they are.''

''I'll figure it out.''

''Quint's secretary might know,'' Greeley offered.

Big Ed stared at her as if he'd never seen her before. Fear uncoiled in Quint's stomach. Could Fern's walking out have triggered a mild stroke? His grandfather looked absolutely shattered. Quint had to do something.

Greeley walked across the room and touched his grandfather's arm. ''Mr. Damian, can I get you a glass of water or anything?''

He patted her hand. ''You're a nice girl. I'm so busy feeling sorry for myself, I forgot about you. She's your mother. Are you okay?'' Big Ed's voice got stronger with each word as he continued to pat Greeley's hand.

Quint watched in amazement as Greeley pushed out her bottom lip and stared down at the floor.

"I'll be all right," she said in a shaky voice. "I'm used to her rejecting me." Her lip wobbled for an instant before Greeley made a visible effort to firm it. "I'm fine. Really I am. I'd better check on dinner." She took a couple of steps and ran into a kitchen chair.

"Are you sure you're okay?" Big Ed moved quickly to her side.

"Something in my eye is all." Wiping her eyes with the back of her hand, she sniffled and gave Big Ed a brave, determined smile.

Quint crossed his arms in front of his chest and leaned back against a kitchen cabinet.

"Don't you worry about dinner," Granddad said. "You sit here and rest. Can I get you something to drink?"

Greeley sat on the chair Big Ed pulled out from the table and gave him a shy smile. "Do you think it would be awful if I had a little wine?"

"Of course not. Quint, get Greeley some wine."

"Oh, I couldn't drink alone. I mean, I'll have a little tiny glass if you will."

Granddad sat down and patted her hand. "Of course I will."

Quint went for goblets. After he had poured the wine, he rolled up his shirtsleeves, checked on the casserole and set the table. Three places. Big Ed was so engrossed in Greeley's highly colorful tales of life on the Nichols ranch, he didn't notice he ate two helpings of the casserole.

Quint resigned himself to his assigned role as chief cook and bottle washer. After he'd stacked the dirty dishes in the dishwasher and turned on the machine, he joined Greeley and his grandfather in the living room, handing his grandfather his usual glass of cognac. Greeley waved away the glass Quint offered her. Big Ed was telling her the details of starting his trucking company. Quint wondered how many women of his acquaintance would have a clue about half of what Big Ed was saying. Greeley hung on Big Ed's every word.

By the time Granddad finally abandoned his easy chair and told Greeley good night, it was far too late for her to drive to Aspen. A fact Quint noted with deep satisfaction.

He waited until he heard his grandfather's bedroom door close, then toasted Greeley with his cognac glass. "You're the biggest liar I ever met."

He thought he might fall in love with her.

CHAPTER NINE

GREELEY EYED QUINT warily, unable to decipher his tone of voice. "Every word I said was true."

"There's truth and there's truth." With a sarcastic lift to his eyebrow, he warbled in a high-pitched voice, "I'm used to rejection. It's just something in my eye. Would it be awful if I had a little wine?"

Her spirits tumbled. She'd expected Quint to understand she'd been trying to drag his grandfather out of his depression. "I am used to rejection," she said in a weary voice.

Quint put down his glass and walked across the room to sit beside her on the sofa. Separating her locked hands, he lifted one and pressed a kiss in her palm. "Thank you."

Greeley's spirits rebounded. "You're welcome," she said in a prim voice, batting her eyelashes at him for effect.

He grinned. "You're as changeable as a chameleon. How am I supposed to know who's the real you?" Leaning back against the sofa, he stretched out his legs and drew Greeley closer to him.

She went willingly, tucking her legs under her as she rested her head against his shoulder. "Maybe you need to undertake an in-depth investigation," she said daringly. Too daringly. An eternity of silence followed her provocative challenge. Quint hadn't been flirting. She'd misinterpreted his gratitude. Her face warmed with embarrassment. "Never mind," she mumbled.

"I don't want to 'never mind.' The trouble is, I can't quite figure out how to interpret what you said. Are you suggesting I get better acquainted with you? Or are you inviting me into your bed?"

Greeley shot upright. "I wasn't inviting you into my bed."

147

"I was afraid of that." He pulled her back against his shoulder. "You're so complex, I don't think I'll live long enough to figure out what makes you tick, but nobody's ever accused me of backing down from a challenge. I'm game if you are."

A variety of emotions rippled through Greeley. Hope, anticipation, pleasure. Sexual awareness. Quint hadn't removed his loosened tie. Greeley tugged at the knot, unable to meet the intensity of his eyes for more than an instant at a time. She could almost hear Worth shouting at her to slow down. "When I was growing up, we used to play in the creek in the home pasture. Beau told me once, kidding around, that there were piranhas in the creek."

"And you believed him," Quint teased.

"Of course not. Not really. And to prove it, I'd race everyone to the creek and jump in first." Quint rhythmically stroked her arm, making it almost possible for her to remember her point. "I thought if there did happen to be an escaped piranha or two in there, if I jumped hard enough, I'd scare them away."

"Are you asking me if I'm a piranha, Ms. Lassiter?"

His stroking slowed, somehow became more intimate. His sexy, playful voice stirred strange and exotic currents deep within her. And battered at her protective gates. She'd never known a man so exciting. So dangerous. Greeley inhaled. "I'm not sure. Are you?"

"I like to think I'm a friendly kind of guy. After all this mess, do you think we can be friends?"

Friends. She'd stupidly hoped for more. Stupid, because Quint had nothing more to offer Fern's daughter. She fixed a smile on her face. "I'd like us to be friends." It wasn't a total lie.

"Friendship is a start."

Hearing the teasing, sensual note in his voice, she risked a peek at his face. The heat in his eyes sizzled through every part of her body. She hung on to his tie for dear life, unable to look away. Then he blinked and the heat had been banked back to harmlessly warm amusement. Not entirely harmless. Greeley wanted to crawl inside his shirt and plaster herself all over his bare chest.

With his arms around her, she'd be safe.

No, not yet. Unknown dangers slithered at the edges of these uncharted waters. Walls could be lowered, gates opened at any time. She didn't have to rush. "To friendship, then. Let's shake on it." She held out a hand, proud she didn't tremble.

"No." With one quick move, Quint pulled her onto his lap. Framing her face with his hands, he said softly, "Let's kiss."

Friends kissed friends. She'd kissed Quint before. Kissing him was safe. Greeley slid her arms around his neck. "All right."

Quint slanted his mouth over hers. She parted her lips, and after only a second's hesitation, slid her tongue over his.

Venturing the tiniest bit out of hiding turned out to have its own rewards.

Quint separated the blinds with his fingers and admired the view. Greeley stood on one of the semi's huge front tires as she leaned over the engine. The truck's raised hood hid her upper body and the mechanic who stood across from her. Quint concentrated on the beautifully shaped rear end tightly encased in worn blue denim and waving in the warm sunshine.

He'd managed to keep her in Denver for three days since they'd sealed their pact with a kiss. He knew she had to get back to Aspen. She had a life there. Family. A career.

He didn't want her to leave.

All's fair in love and war, he told himself, and when the sculpture wasn't enough, he threw Big Ed's fragile health at her. The trouble was, he didn't know if this was love or war. Or both.

It was definitely a war of sorts. Fighting his way through all those thick walls she'd erected around herself. The night she'd kissed him to seal their getting-to-know-you pact had given him a false sense of accomplishment. Three days later he knew what she liked when he kissed her. He knew little more about the real Greeley.

He knew he wanted her. Body and soul.

He told himself she'd give herself to him when she was ready.

When she trusted him enough.

Some women were worth waiting for.

Quint shoved his impatience back in its cubby hole. Last night had been the worst yet. Each time she came willingly into his arms only fired his blood for more.

He didn't know what kind of music she liked, her favorite food, how she voted. He knew she was close to the family who'd raised her, liked animals, was incredibly talented and mechanically gifted.

He knew he wanted to drag her off the truck, throw her in his car, speed home and lock her into his bedroom until he'd slowly and thoroughly laid bare every one of her secrets.

Then he could ask her if she preferred Chinese food or Mexican food.

"If you'd pull those blinds all the way open and turn your desk around you could watch her all day long," Beth said tartly.

"Isn't it about time for you to retire so I can hire someone young and pretty who isn't always mouthing off at me?"

His secretary joined him at the window. "I was wrong about her. She's nothing like Fern. Down-to-earth, practical, friendly, helpful. She took care of canceling most of the wedding arrangements." Beth heaved a big sigh. "And the way she looks in those jeans makes me pea-green with envy."

"Ah. Jack planning to run away with her?"

"Not if you do it first," she said sharply and left.

More footsteps entered in her wake and his grandfather

stood at his shoulder. "I sure do like that girl. Do you believe she actually knows what a fuel solenoid is? You'd be a fool to let her get away."

Quint took one last look at Greeley's enticing rear end and returned to his desk. "Maybe she doesn't want to stay."

Big Ed laughed. "Bribe her with your dad's car. She really loves that car." He sat in the chair across the desk from Quint. "You notice the way she runs her hand over the fender when she thinks no one's looking?"

He'd noticed. And wished she'd run her hand over him the same way. Quint placed his hands on his desk and leaned back in his chair. If he didn't quit thinking about Greeley Lassiter in his bed, trucking in and out of Denver was going to take a sharp drop. "I talked to Russ Gordon this morning. He's balking at the new contract. I thought maybe you could persuade him."

Big Ed gave him a keen-eyed look. "You keeping the old man busy to heal his broken heart?"

So much for trying to be subtle. "Do I need to?"

"Nope. Greeley's right. Fern gave us what she had to give. It's not her fault we wanted more. Greeley got a family, and I got a couple of months of pretty hot and heavy sex. Things sure have changed since my day. Boy howdy, what Fern taught me!"

Quint knocked his fountain pen on the floor and went down on his hands and knees in a pretense of searching for it. He didn't want to discuss sexual techniques with his grandfather. A second later, he popped his head above the level of his desk. "You haven't been discussing your's and Fern's bedroom activities with Greeley, have you?"

Big Ed looked at him in disgust. "I'm old, not senile."

"Sorry." Quint resumed his seat.

"You going to marry her?"

The pen went flying to the floor again. "It's too soon to think about that," Quint said stiffly.

His grandfather raised a white bush of an eyebrow. "Don't

blow it. A woman like her isn't going to hang around forever waiting for you to make up your mind. If I were forty years younger, I'd give you a run for your money."

"As I recall, you weren't interested in advice from me when you started seeing Fern."

His grandfather snorted. "I suppose that's a fancy way of telling me to mind my own business. You can't expect patience out of a man pushing eighty. I want to hold my great-grandkids and spoil them rotten." Big Ed poked at a spot on his thumb and said in an overly casual voice, "Maybe I should have spoiled you more and not expected so much from you."

Trying to picture children with a combination of his and Greeley's genes, his grandfather's words didn't immediately sink in. When they did, Quint asked, "Where does that come from?"

"You work too hard. You ought to play more. Take Greeley up in the mountains. Fishing or something."

"I've never been fishing in my life."

"We should have fished." Big Ed sighed. "Hiked. Done the stuff a man does with a boy."

"We did. We played with trucks."

"I raised you to run Damian Trucking." His grandfather stood and stared over Quint's head for a long moment, obviously lost in thought. Then he stirred and wiped his hand over his face. "Seventy-six years is a long time to live. A man makes choices, some good, some bad. Trouble is, by the time you figure out which is which, it's too late. You can't go back. Still, a man has to go on trying. Doing what seems best." Big Ed turned and walked out of the office.

Quint settled back in his chair and chewed on the tip of his retrieved pen. What was that all about? Was his grandfather starting to hear mortality creeping up?

Greeley sat in the worn leather chair in Quint's office and watched him over the top of her sketch pad. After dinner

Edward Damian had gone to his room to watch television, and Quint was catching up on the logjam of paperwork which had resulted from his trip to Aspen. Theoretically she was sketching ideas for the sculpture he wanted. In truth, she was admiring Quint's squared jaw and chin, so indicative of his strength.

She could almost feel the rasp of his five-o'clock shadow against her face. She loved that feel. Loved the way he concentrated on what he was doing.

Concentrated so hard he forgot she sat across the room.

"Jack let me help him repair the exhaust system on Tony's rig today," she said to the room at large. She'd watched while Jack did the repair.

Quint looked up. "I'll tell Tony to increase his insurance." His gaze went back to his paperwork.

Greeley loved the way he scratched Barney's stomach with his foot while he read. She loved his freshly laundered shirts and expensive trousers and Italian loafers.

She loved his smile.

Loved the way he kissed.

"You're jealous because Jack won't let you near an engine."

Quint lowered his papers and gave her an odd look. "Did Jack say that?"

"He doesn't have to. A person can look at you and tell you don't know an alternator from an air compressor."

"A person can, can she?"

"Come on, Quint, those hands have never changed a fan belt, much less a fuel filter."

"Is that so?" he asked in an annoyed voice.

She hadn't meant to slight his manhood. "It's no big deal. You're the boss. You don't have to know how. Your job is hiring people who can do it." She gave him an encouraging smile.

He tossed his papers aside and stalked over to her. Taking

her sketch pad out of her hands, he carefully laid it on his desk, then braced his hands on the arms of her chair.

"I have a degree in business from the University of Colorado."

"There, see? Exactly what you need to run a business," she said cheerfully.

He bared his teeth at her. "I am also certified as a Master Heavy-Duty Truck Technician by ASE. For the ignorant, that's the National Institute for Automotive Service Excellence."

The ends of his tie hung down in front of her. Greeley wrapped them around her fists and gave him what she hoped was a sultry smile, "Well, since you're a master mechanic, do you know anything about engines?"

His eyes gleamed. "I might."

"I think mine's running a little rough."

Quint pulled her to her feet. "As a master mechanic, I can get you purring in no time."

As a master mechanic, he didn't make false promises.

Quint whistled as he walked down the hall from his bedroom. He'd heard Big Ed up earlier, and the smell of coffee wafted from the kitchen. "Good morning."

His grandfather lifted his mug of coffee in greeting. "Coffee's done," he said unnecessarily.

Quint grabbed a mug and filled it. "Looks like it's going to be a beautiful day." He wished the most beautiful part of his day would hurry up and walk into the kitchen.

"It's raining," his grandfather said dryly.

"We need the rain. Saves on our water bill."

"I saw that mountain of paperwork you had last night. I feel bad I let things go while you were in Aspen. Get it done?"

"Not quite. I got a little distracted." More than a little distracted. Quint's body tightened at the memory of Greeley sitting in his lap. He stared into his coffee. Not sitting.

Writhing, he thought with satisfaction. Especially when he'd tasted her breasts. He took a gulp of hot coffee and reached for a box of cereal. If he didn't think of something else, in a minute he'd be writhing himself. Putting his bowl of cereal on the kitchen table, he sat across from his grandfather.

Big Ed clutched his mug of coffee with both hands. "I wanted to talk to you before you go to work this morning."

Something in his grandfather's voice made Quint stop eating and put down his spoon. "Sure, shoot."

"You probably guessed I intended to give Fern a share of the business as a wedding present." Big Ed paused. "I hoped she would help you after I passed on. Expecting you to run the whole shebang is asking a lot of you."

"Damian Trucking is my life."

Big Ed gave him a fleeting smile. "You work too hard. I've been thinking." He avoided looked directly at Quint. "I was darned selfish and thoughtless when it came to Greeley. I knew Fern was getting restless, and I thought if I reunited her with her daughter, Fern would be so grateful, she'd stay with me. I used Greeley to bribe Fern."

Quint should have realized his grandfather's conscience bothered him. "Don't worry about it. Greeley understands." He picked up his spoon and resumed eating.

"She's been an awful good sport about it," Big Ed agreed, "especially considering I didn't give a darn about her feelings. I was having a good time with Fern in my bed, and I was willing to use Greeley to make sure Fern stayed in my bed."

Unable to think of a response, Quint continued eating.

"I wish I'd never sent you to Aspen after Greeley, but I did. Can't change that." Big Ed looked down at his coffee. "The only thing I can do is try and make amends. If Fern and I had married, Greeley would eventually have inherited her mother's share of the company. So it seems right she gets it now."

Quint knocked his cereal bowl over. Ignoring the milk spilling to the floor, he stared at his grandfather. "What?"

"You heard me. Greeley ought to be part-owner of Damian Trucking. One way or the other."

The paperwork on the desk mocked Quint's superficial calm. He'd managed to finish breakfast, speak civilly to his grandfather and to Greeley when she'd appeared in the kitchen. He had no idea what he'd said. A few employees had given him some strange looks shortly after he'd arrived at the terminal, but nobody asked questions, so he hadn't made too big a fool of himself.

Quint curled his mouth in derision. When it came to fools, he led the pack.

He was as bad as his grandfather. Thinking with something other than his brains. From the second he'd seen Greeley standing in the doorway at the Gilded Lily in Aspen he'd wanted to bed her. To justify his lust, he'd convinced himself he cared for her.

A man so easily distracted by a deceitful woman didn't deserve to inherit the entire business.

His office door opened and Greeley popped her head in. "Hi." She looked deceptively innocent. And desirable.

"I'm kind of busy right now," he said tightly.

"This will just take a second. Jack was telling me about an auto salvage place, and I thought I'd run over there and check it out. I wondered if I could borrow your car to go back to the house to get my pickup."

"I don't loan my car to just anyone who walks in off the street."

Greeley went very still. "I didn't realize I was just someone off the street," she finally said.

Quint pressed his palms flat on top his desk. She could give acting lessons to an award-winning actress. It was her bad luck that he wasn't as big a pushover as his grandfather. She couldn't fool him. Not anymore.

"I started coming down here before I could walk," he said. "By the time I started school I knew the names of most of the tools. By the time I was in high school I could change fuel filters, water pumps, you name it. At fourteen I started going out on the road with some of the drivers during school vacations. The rest of the year I unloaded freight or helped in the shop. At eighteen I qualified for a commercial driver's licence that was good in Colorado. As soon as I turned twenty-one I qualified for a CDL, good for driving anywhere in the United States. I was raised to run Damian Trucking."

Greeley walked into the office. "If this is about my teasing you last night about not being mechanically minded, I—"

"It's my fault. I shouldn't blame you."

She sat in the other chair. "Blame me for what?"

Her guileless face didn't deceive him for an instant. "You warned me. Told me straight out you came to Denver to ruin my plans, that you intended to make sure Fern married Granddad so she'd inherit a big share of the trucking company. How did you know Big Ed intended to give her part of the company as a wedding gift? Or was that just a lucky guess on your part?

"You're Fern's only child. You figured you'd eventually inherit. It must have come as quite a shock when Fern walked away from the company. Up until then, you'd just been toying with me, killing time until you could charm your way into your mother's heart. But Fern has no heart, and with her gone, your plans changed. You'd get the company through me."

Quint jammed his tight fists into trouser pockets. "Didn't I move fast enough for you? Is that why you decided to work on Big Ed instead? He'd proved he was a sap for Fern. Why not Fern's daughter? You wormed your way into his affection. Stole one of the few things I cared about."

He'd cared about her. No, he refused to think about that.

"I don't know what you're—"

"No, you didn't know. Here's how big a dope I am. I was

going to ask you to marry me. I didn't want to rush you. That's pretty funny, now that I think about it. You were playing hard to get, manipulating me to get what you wanted. I thought Fern was bad, but she could learn a lot from you.''

Greeley slowly stood. ''I have no idea what this is about. All I know is you've judged me and pronounced me guilty of something, because I'm Fern's daughter. You couldn't get past my mongrel pedigree, could you?''

''What I couldn't get past was wanting you in my bed and you know it.''

She took a step back.

The look on her face infuriated him. She had no right to pretend she was devastated. Quint stormed around his desk and grabbed her chin. ''You can stop acting,'' he sneered. ''You've won. Big Ed always wanted a granddaughter. And a grandson like his son. He didn't get either. That's life, baby. Tell Big Ed I don't want Damian Trucking. Not all of it. Not half of it. Not any of it. You can have the whole damned thing.''

''Me?'' Staring at him, she made no attempt to break free of his grasp. ''Are you crazy?''

''Not anymore. You told me once to start my own trucking business, and that's exactly what I intend to do. And then, Ms. Lassiter, I'm going to put you and Damian Trucking out of business.''

He hated those eyes filling her face. Hated the way she pretended to be innocent. The color of her eyes would be perfect for painting his trucks when he got his own business up and running. Blue and gray to remind him what a fool he'd been. He was still a fool. He wanted to kiss her.

He wasn't that big a fool.

He'd already proved he was. Tightening his grip on her chin, Quint came down on her mouth like a rig running at top speed. He kissed her deep and he kissed her long. She didn't fight him. They were both panting hard when he finally lifted his head.

She made no other sound as he walked away.

Greeley couldn't have uttered a word if her life depended on it. Shock, confusion, betrayal and innumerable other emotions too ephemeral to label muddled her head and squeezed her heart. The agonizing pain would come later, once she let herself think about what had just happened. She wouldn't think.

"Here. You wanted these. Take them," Quint said savagely from behind her.

She refused to turn around. Something flew past her ear, and car keys landed with a loud clatter on Quint's desk.

"The car belonged to my father. No doubt Big Ed wants to give it to you, too. He was going on yesterday about how much you wanted it," Quint added with a sneer.

The door banged behind him.

She stood paralyzed. If she so much as blinked an eyelid, she'd break into a million pieces. Excruciating pain assaulted her. If she only knew why...

He hated her. His eyes had been black with anger and hate, his mouth curled with contempt. He'd hurled angry, hateful accusations at her. Accusations which made no sense.

He'd kissed her in anger. To show her how much he hated her.

No. He'd wanted to kiss her that way, but he hadn't. Somewhere, on some level, she'd recognized the difference. And responded.

The intensity in his kiss had broken through all her barriers. She didn't respond to anger.

She responded to his deep hurt, his need.

Someone, something had hurt Quint so deeply he'd lashed out at her. Greeley knew all about that kind of pain.

The door opened behind her. She didn't dare turn. Not until all her walls were in place.

"Quint's secretary came rushing out to the shop. She said

Quint walked out, told her he was quitting. What's going on?''

Slowly Greeley turned to face Edward. "I don't know."

He gave her a sharp look. "What's wrong? You two have a fight?''

She shook her head. "Quint said to tell you…" Her voice failed. It wasn't as if she'd forgotten Quint's message. The words were burned into her brain. Taking a deep breath, she tried again. "His exact words were, 'Tell Big Ed I don't want Damian Trucking. Not all of it. Not half of it. Not any of it. You can have the whole damned thing.' Quint meant me. That I could have the business. What do I have to do with any of this?''

Quint's grandfather stared at her, her inner shock written on his face. "It's my fault. I wanted him to marry you. I gave him some pretty broad hints yesterday, but although he admitted he liked you, he seemed a little skittish about the idea of marriage. I thought maybe he was a little too comfortable with being a bachelor so I'd thought I'd give him a little shove.''

Edward's words made no sense. He'd talked to Quint yesterday about marriage, but Quint had kissed her last night. She'd felt safe in his arms. Convinced herself he was coming to love her. "He wasn't angry last night." Greeley buried deep the memory of Quint's outraged face as he had sneered that he'd been going to ask her to marry him. She'd deal with that pain in private.

Edward walked over to the window and stood with his back to her. "It was this morning at breakfast. I'm sure he loves you, but he doesn't know it yet. I thought I'd give him some reasons for marrying you.''

Deep foreboding twisted Greeley's middle. "Like what?''

"Told him I felt guilty about how I'd treated you. That you'd be great as part-owner of this place.''

Appalled, Greeley stared at Edward's back. "You actually thought you could blackmail him into marrying me by giving me a piece of Damian Trucking? Did you think he'd marry me to get it back?''

Edward swung around. "Who said anything about giving you part of Damian Trucking? When a man and woman marry, they become partners. I've watched you. Everything about this place interests you. You'd understand the demands of the business, be able to help Quint out.''

Greeley made her way on shaking legs to Quint's desk and sat on the edge. "He thought you were taking part of the company away from him and giving it to me.''

"Why would I do something that dumb? I built this business to pass on to my son and grandson.''

"Quint seemed to think you planned to give part of it to Fern as a wedding present.''

"So she'd stick around after I was gone, to help Quint out. I know how demanding this business is. Heck, Eddie, Quint's father, didn't want anything to do with it. Too much work for him. Too much dirt. Not glamorous enough. I worked hard to give my son everything he ever wanted. Spoiled him." His voice changed. "I didn't want to make that same mistake with Quint so I made him work for everything he got.''

Edward pulled a large white handkerchief out of his pocket and noisily blew his nose. "I've always been proud of how my grandson turned out.''

"Did you ever tell him that?''

"Didn't have to. Men don't need all that mushy stuff. Quint knows how I feel about him.''

Greeley thought of the trophy wall in their living room. "Edward," she said gently, "I don't think Quint has a clue. All I've heard about since I've been in Denver is how wonderful Quint's father was. You're both his heroes. Quint must feel as if he's never measured up to either one of you.''

"That's ridiculous. So what if he's not a hero or never saved any lives?''

She gave the elderly man a look of incredulity. And then

told him in no uncertain terms how wrong he was. She pointed out the many ways a man could save another's life. Undramatic ways, but nonetheless vital ways.

When she'd finished, Edward looked as if he'd been run over by one of his eighteen-wheelers. "I think I'd better go after that boy and tell him I've been a fool all these years." His voice strengthened. "And then I'll tell him he can't walk out on me. He's got a company to run."

Quint could walk out. And had. He'd whistled down a big rig rolling out of the terminal yard and jumped into the passenger seat.

According to the dispatcher, the truck and Quint were on their way to Albuquerque, New Mexico.

The bright sunlight hurt Quint's eyes.

After asking if Quint had a problem with his driving and receiving a negative answer, Warren kept his mouth shut. When his cell phone rang, he answered it and handed the phone to Quint, but said nothing when Quint hung up without speaking. They'd ignored the ringing phone when it immediately rang again. It didn't stop ringing for a long time.

Quint had left his sunglasses in his car. Leaning his head back, he closed his eyes, blocking out the sun. If only the memories of Greeley could be blocked out as easily.

The taste of her mouth lingered on his lips. Her scent had marked his clothes, his skin. Invisible strands mocking his gullibility.

She'd denied nothing.

Pretended she had no idea what he was talking about.

Fern's daughter. He'd persuaded himself he'd been wrong about her. That conniving didn't run in her blood.

Warren pulled out of the Port of Entry on I-25 and smoothly merged with the heavy traffic heading south toward Colorado Springs.

"I never understood how Fern could fool Big Ed so completely," Quint said out loud.

Warren darted a quick look at him. "She's a looker."

"Like her daughter."

"Nah. My wife sells make-up in a department store. She said Fern knew every trick in the trade about hiding bad stuff and bringing out good. Greeley, now, she's natural. A nice kid with a great smile."

She'd fooled Warren, too. And the rest of the drivers and the mechanics and the people who worked in the office and the salesmen. Did stupidity, like misery, love company?

Not that Quint was miserable.

The interstate highway crossed from Colorado into New Mexico, crawled up and over Raton Pass, and curved its way down toward Santa Fe. An easy run in good weather. No hidden dangers as in the past. No huge boulders on the trail. No bandits or Comanche war parties. No tollgates.

No Greeley Lassiter to catch you unawares with her "great smile." Okay, she did have a great smile. Her smiles had captivated everyone at Damian Trucking. Even his dog had been wild about her. Which meant nothing. It was easy enough to fool Barney. Just scratch behind his ears.

Barney had avoided Fern.

They left the outskirts of Santa Fe in the rearview mirror. "A woman ever make a fool of you?" Quint asked Warren.

"You and Greeley have a fight?"

"What made you think of her? Did everyone know she was making a fool of me?"

Warren gave him an incredulous look. "Greeley wouldn't know how to break a man's heart."

"Who said anything about my heart? My heart isn't the least bit involved."

"When you wouldn't talk to the old man on my cell phone, I thought you and him had had words. Guess you and Greeley had a lover's quarrel, huh?"

"We were never lovers," Quint said stiffly.

Warren laughed. "You might fire me for saying this, boss, but her eyes make love to you every time she looks at you.

The mechanics have a pool going on when you'll propose."
He added casually, "I have five bucks riding on this week-
end."

"You can kiss your five bucks goodbye."

Her eyes didn't make love.

Okay, so it was possible they went all warm and mushy
when he kissed her. Leading him on.

When he'd yelled at her, her eyes had turned the dull,
leaden blue of skies before a storm. Gloomy, ominous skies
which were followed more often than not by the kind of
tragedies nature unleashed upon the innocent. Quint had seen
the same stunned look of disbelief in the eyes of victims
when he'd driven emergency food and medical supplies to
disaster areas.

He'd felt sorry for those people. Felt guilty they'd been
left with so little when he had so much. Felt guilty he
couldn't do more for them.

He didn't feel guilty about Greeley.

Who was he kidding? Sickening remorse sat leaden in his
stomach. He felt as if he'd slapped a baby.

Greeley was nothing like her mother. He'd been insanely
wrong to turn on her the way he had.

Even if she fooled the whole world, she couldn't fool him.
She'd allowed him too many peeks into her soul. Her only
lies were for protection. The bold, aggressive facade hiding
an inner fear of being hurt. Of being abandoned.

The way he'd abandoned her. Hardly the action of a hero.

She deserved better. A man who'd proved himself. A man
who'd done more in life than be born in line to inherit a
business. She needed—deserved—a hero.

He'd walked away from Damian Trucking. He had nothing
to offer her.

After he got his own trucking company going would be
too late. By then she would have fallen in love. With someone else.

Greeley didn't love him. Warren could spout all the nonsense in the world about her eyes making love to Quint, and it wouldn't make it true.

If she loved him, Quint would know.

CHAPTER TEN

"WHAT'S HE DOING in California? I thought he was in Texas."

Greeley studied the hubcap she'd earlier welded to the sculpture before she answered Cheyenne's question. "He was. Now he's in Los Angeles." Damian Trucking drivers used satellite communication to stay in contact with the home terminal, which meant that Warren contacted the dispatcher who reported to Edward who called Greeley.

"I can't believe he's been gone a week and you haven't heard from him beyond one measly postcard. Did he tell you when he'd see you again?"

"No." Greeley clamped her jaws together to keep from shrieking with pain. After a second, she continued. "He apologized for some things he'd said and wished me good luck."

Cheyenne looked around the shop and sat gingerly on an old stool. "Mom said you haven't said much about what happened in Denver." The unspoken question hung in the air.

Greeley shot her oldest sister a mocking look. "I'll bet Thomas told you to mind your own business." At Cheyenne's nod, Greeley added tartly, "And yet, here you are."

"Here I are," Cheyenne agreed in a composed voice. "You came home from Denver and announced Fern's wedding was off. When prodded, you added Quint had walked out on his grandfather, and then you holed up in here. Leaving your family to worry themselves sick. Worry's bad for pregnant women."

"There's nothing for you to worry about."

"You're wearing red."

Greeley cast an elaborate look at her faded brown coveralls. "I didn't realize pregnancy caused color-blindness."

Cheyenne waved off the sarcastic comment. "You're wearing your tough-guy, no-one-can-hurt-me attitude." Her voice gentled. "I know Fern dumped you again, but she's not your real family, so nobody cares about that, which means the problem must be Quint."

Greeley pulled her safety headgear into place, switched on the electric grinder and buffed a section of her sculpture.

Her sister waited. Greeley knew from long experience Cheyenne Lassiter Steele would not leave until she had some answers.

Repressing a sigh, Greeley turned off the grinder and removed her headgear. The whir of the grinder died away while she considered how much to tell her sister.

The whine of a tractor rode a small gust of wind into the shop. The breeze added the dry smell of dust to the pungent odors of the workshop.

"He never trusted me," Greeley finally said. "Because of Fern. Because she gave birth to me, he thought I must be like her, or at least aligned with her against him."

"That's stupid."

"Yes, well..." Greeley shrugged. "He wrote on the postcard he'd been wrong about that and apologized."

"But? What's the rest of it?"

Greeley found a burr she'd failed to grind smooth and poked it with her finger, welcoming the sharp sensation of pain. "I think he loves me, but I also think he doesn't believe he's worthy of being loved." Once started, she couldn't stop.

"You should see their house. The living room is a shrine to Quint's father. It bothered me, because there's nothing anywhere of Quint's, but at first I missed the significance of that. After Edward implied he'd been disappointed in his son, I asked a few questions of people who'd been with Damian Trucking for years. None of them liked Quint's father. Said he was one of those people who did well at everything, and he started acting as if he were better than everyone else. He believed it was his right to be on top, and he only had time for those he thought could put him there.''

Cheyenne frowned at her. ''The man died saving other people. Surely...''

''Edward has awful doubts about that,'' Greeley said. ''He never told a single soul this, but after Quint left, Edward confessed to me he believes his son went back to the plane because he knew it would earn him a medal and look good on his record. Edward doesn't think it ever occurred to his son that he wouldn't survive.''

''That's a terrible thing to say about your own son.''

''I know. So does Edward, and it tears him up inside. He blames himself for raising his son to be self-centered and, well, snobbish. He was determined to raise Quint differently.''

''You spent a lot of time with Quint. Did Edward succeed?''

''Too well. Edward said he didn't praise Quint, not wanting him to get a swelled head. Instead, whatever Quint accomplished, Edward told him he could do better and reminded him his dad had given the ultimate sacrifice. As if that stupid shrine wasn't enough of a reminder. He never told Quint the truth about his father. Quint thinks his dad was perfect, a hero, and that he can never measure up. Edward even had the nerve to tell me Quint wasn't a hero, that he'd never saved a life.''

''Is he your hero?'' Cheyenne studied Greeley's face. ''Do you love him?''

''He's made a difference in so many people's lives. And done things I'd never have known about if I hadn't gone to Denver. He adopted this silly little short-legged beagle who idolizes him, and he knows more about engines than I'll ever know—he's even a certified master mechanic and he has a commercial driver's license, and everyone respects him so much as their boss, and he's so good to his grandfather and…'' She broke off as Cheyenne started laughing. Except she had one last confession to make, ''…and I don't mind when he kisses me.''

''I knew it was true love as soon as you said 'master mechanic,''' Cheyenne teased. ''Go up to Denver and when he gets back, tell him you love him.''

Greeley shook her head. ''I could tell Quint until I'm blue in the face how much I love him, but I'd be wasting my breath. He has to learn for himself that he can trust my love.''

''Did you ever tell him you love him?''

Greeley picked up a hammer. ''Maybe not in so many words.'' She pounded out a dent. ''I showed him in a hundred ways.''

Cheyenne eased off the stool and stopped Greeley's swinging arm. ''Dear sister of mine, you are an idiot.''

Quint wondered what she'd thought when she'd read the postcard. He'd bought more postcards, tried to write her again, but utterly failed at finding the right words. No explanation excused his behavior.

He'd been simple-minded to the point of being pigheaded. Prejudging her based on an accident of birth. And then, after he'd come to know her, he'd flown in the face of everything he'd learned about her and accused her of treachery.

Despite her blustery claims when she came to Denver he'd sensed at the time she was merely spitting in the wind. Every move she'd made in Denver had confirmed his suspicions that her hard-nosed attitude was a total sham. Greeley Lassiter simply didn't have an aptitude for revenge.

He didn't doubt she'd been hurt by him and by Fern and wanted to hurt back. Her problem was, remorse followed too quickly on the heels of her anger. Forget her tough facade. Greeley was too soft, too good, and too kind to enjoy the fruits of revenge.

He knew her true character because she'd trusted him enough to cautiously lower her protective shield and allow him partial entry. He'd destroyed that trust through accusations he'd known were unfounded before he left Denver.

Grandfather had made it clear he didn't trust Quint to handle Damian Trucking alone. Big Ed's assessment had blindsided him, but taking the hurt and anger out on Greeley had been dead wrong.

Quint rubbed a weary hand over his face. New Mexico, Texas, California, Arizona and back to Colorado. The states blurred in his mind. Superimposed on the landscape had always been Greeley's face. Sometimes laughing. Sometimes reaching for a kiss. Mostly looking as she'd looked when he'd walked out on her. Disbelieving and hurt. Shell-shocked.

The devastated look on her face would haunt him the rest of his days. And his nights.

He'd apologized in his postcard. It wasn't enough. It would never be enough.

If only he could take her in his arms and beg her forgiveness, beg her to let him spend the rest of his life making up for his insults. Tell her how much he loved her.

He couldn't. Not now.

When a man loved a woman, he did what was best for her. Greeley was better off without him. What did he have to offer her? A company that was little more than jottings on an envelope and a willingness to work hard.

Now that it was too late to profit by the lesson, he'd learned how little Damian Trucking meant to him compared to the people in his life. He'd been too willing to sacrifice another's happiness. A man who put ownership of Damian Trucking ahead of his grandfather's happiness, ahead of Greeley's well-being, deserved to lose the business.

In his darkest moments he wondered if his claims that his actions were motivated by concern for his grandfather were nothing more than justification for his own selfish behavior.

He'd rolled over Greeley's reluctance to meet her mother like an eighteen-wheeler over an empty cardboard box.

No wonder she didn't love him.

If only a man could erase the past and start over. He'd be the kind of man she could love.

The truck lurched sideways, and Warren swore, fighting to bring the truck back on the highway. "Idiot!"

Jerked from his thoughts, Quint looked up to see a white pickup speeding erratically down the highway. He grabbed Warren's cell phone and called the police, then held his breath as the pickup careened around a knot of slower-moving vehicles farther down the road.

The white pickup almost succeeded in passing safely. At the last second it clipped a car and started a chain-reaction of accidents. By the time Warren brought his big rig to a standstill on the side of the highway, they were almost on top of the massive pile-up.

Flames licked at one of the crunched smaller cars. The crash must have ruptured the fuel tank. Yelling at Warren to grab the fire extinguisher, Quint leapt from the high cab of the semi and raced toward the car. A small face looked out the back seat window. The front window was missing enough glass for Quint to reach in and unlock the doors. A man lay slumped over the steering wheel. Two children cried in the back.

Others ran up. Leaving the driver to them, Quint wrenched open the back door and unbuckled the nearest child's seat belt. Handing the little boy to a man behind him, Quint ducked into the car for the second child. The boy fought him, slapping at Quint. The gas tank could explode any second. He didn't have time to persuade the child. Unbuckling the seat belt, Quint grabbed the kid and bolted from the car.

The little boy beat on Quint's chest, screaming at Quint. "Put me down! I gotta get Suzie. Suzie's in the car."

Quint's blood ran cold. He hadn't seen a third child. There wasn't time to go after her. Thrusting the boy at the nearest person, Quint dashed back to the wreck. He couldn't find the girl. "Suzie? Suzie, where are you? Come on, honey, your dad and brothers want you to come with them? Suzie?"

A noise came from under the front seat. Leaning down, Quint came nose-to-nose with Suzie. He reached for her and got his hand scratched for his trouble. Ignoring the pain, he swept Suzie from under the seat and headed for safety. The tank exploded before he'd taken three running steps.

His last thought was that he'd never told Greeley he loved her.

The phone rang in the workshop. Studying the finished sculpture through half-closed eyes, Greeley ignored the phone. It continued to ring stridently. With a sigh she picked it up. When Edward finished talking, Greeley said politely, "Thank you for calling," and carefully disconnected.

She staggered over to the stool, her body numb, her thoughts a chaotic jumble of grief and disbelief and self-pity and rage. How dare Quint do this to her?

"Mom called down to the barn and told me. Edward phoned the house first." Worth stood in the doorway.

Greeley gestured helplessly. If she opened her mouth to speak, she'd disintegrate.

"Hop in the shower and get cleaned up. Mom's calling Cheyenne. She'll arrange transportation. Thomas must know someone with a private jet parked at the airport. If not, I'll drive you to Colorado Springs."

"Colorado Springs?" Her voice came out a croak.

"That's where they took Quint."

"Oh." Greeley looked down at her hands. The sympathy in Worth's eyes underlined her pain. And destroyed any hope of miracles. A smear of rust colored one knuckle. She rubbed at it. "Cheyenne says I'm stupid because I didn't tell him I loved him."

"You can tell him now."

"It's a little late." The tears came then. A torrent of tears. "Allie said it's always about pride with me. That I make people prove they love me. That I test their love. She said love is more important than pride. That loving and being loved is all there is, and life's too short not to love."

Accepting Worth's handkerchief, Greeley blew her nose. Nothing stopped her tears. "I didn't know how short. I thought there'd be time." Reaching out blindly, she felt the smooth, cold metal. "I thought when he saw this, he'd know. Now it's too late. Too late." She pounded the sculpture with her fist, welcoming the pain which shot through her knuckles. "He's dead. He had no right to die and leave me."

Worth pulled her off the stool and into his arms. Holding her close, he repeated the same words over and over again. Repeated them until they penetrated Greeley's anguish.

She leaned back, staring at him. Worth wouldn't lie to her. "He's not dead?" she managed to choke out.

"Burns, badly broken leg, assorted cuts and bruises, but definitely alive. He's in surgery now, getting his leg bones pinned together."

"He's alive," Greeley repeated dumbly. If Worth hadn't been holding her, she would have collapsed. "Alive." She smiled at him through a blurred curtain of salt water, but she, who never cried, couldn't stop crying.

"I swear," Worth said in mock disgust, squeezing the breath from her. "How hard can it be to fall in love without making a big mess of it? What did Edward Damian tell you?"

"An accident...Quint...blew up." Waterlogged gulps for air punctuated her words. "After that...my mind shut down." Overwhelming relief and euphoria swept over her. "He's alive!" She shook loose from her brother's arms. "I have to go." Running toward the house, she skidded to a stop in the middle of the yard. "Worth! Don't just stand there! Help me. I have to get to Colorado Springs."

He'd awakened before. Long enough to see his grandfather standing by the bed. Big Ed had said the man and his kids would be okay, then launched on a rambling apology. Somewhere in the middle of it, waves of pain swamped him, and his grandfather had yelled for a nurse, and someone had come and Quint had sunk into blessed oblivion.

The next time his mom and Phil were there, Phil telling his mom not to worry, that Quint was in good hands. Quint wanted to tell them his leg hurt, not his hands, but he drifted off again.

Now his eyelids were too heavy to open. His leg ached, but the screaming pain had quieted to a dull roar. Quint's mind wandered aimlessly until the sound of turning pages broke through his tangled thoughts.

He wasn't alone. Someone sat by his bed. His mother. Or his grandfather.

If he opened his eyes, he'd know. Opening his eyes took too much effort. Using his other senses, Quint played a guessing game.

Big Ed breathed too heavily to be his visitor.

His mother had worn a heavy, old-fashioned scent from the time his father had given her a bottle of it, saying it was his favorite perfume. Quint took a deep breath. Not his mother.

That left a nurse.

The scent of wildflowers teased his nostrils.

He was a city boy. He didn't even know how wildflowers smelled.

The fragrance brought an image to his mind. A calendar picture. A field of wildflowers. Natural beauty. Flowers looking impossibly fragile against a wild, mountain backdrop. Sturdy flowers which bloomed where nature planted them.

Greeley.

Quint refused to open his eyes in case he'd guessed wrong.

"If you think I'll go away because you're pretending you're asleep, it's not going to happen."

He forced his eyelids up. "What are you doing here?"

She stood and moved closer to the bed. "Looking for a

place to kiss. You took half the skin off your face when you skidded across the road.''

He closed his eyes. The look in hers frightened him. Gave him hope. He refused to hope. ''That's not what I meant.''

She pressed a cool—no, it was warm—kiss on his temple. ''What I'm doing is sitting here reading about you in the newspaper. Denver man injured while rescuing a father and two sons from a burning car.''

''I was just the first person there. Plenty of others helped.'' Quint wondered if she knew how hard she was clinging to his fingers.

''What about Suzie? You're a hero. Hannah sent you a picture she drew of you and the cat being blown out of the burning car.''

He thought he heard amusement in her voice. ''I'm no hero. I thought Suzie was a little girl. Not a stupid cat. I hate cats.''

''I won't tell Hannah. She might refuse to be flower girl at our wedding.''

His eyes shot back open. ''What wedding?''

''Ours.'' She fiddled with his sheet, unnecessarily straightening it. ''Since your mom and Phil are here, I was all for marrying you here in your hospital bed, but Cheyenne said she's running this wedding and there will be no bedside ceremonies and no brides in blue jeans.''

''You're marrying me?''

''Who else would I marry? Your surgeon's pretty cute, but I think he's already married.''

''I never asked you to marry me.''

Her gaze flashed over his face and locked on the IV stand beside his bed. ''You said you would have only Edward interfered and now you won't because you think I'd think you were asking because you think Edward was planning to give me part of Damian Trucking but all Edward was doing was trying to spur you on to propose to me because he wants great-grandchildren.'' She stopped to breathe.

Quint looked blankly at her. Sorting out what she'd said and what she meant muddled his aching head. He closed his eyes.

His brain had painted her image on his eyelids. Bare arms and shoulders. A bare midriff. And in between the exposed areas of flesh, a blood-red puckered tube thing which clung tightly to her every curve.

One thought popped out of a discordant jumble of thoughts.

For all her confident words about weddings, Greeley Lassiter was scared spitless.

For some reason, which he was too tired to analyze, Quint found the idea oddly comforting.

The room was too warm, intensifying the hospital smells.

Greeley told herself sleep was healing. Didn't it knit bones or something? Yet each time Quint fell sleep, panic clawed at her throat. She'd come so close to losing him. Gingerly she felt for his pulse. It beat strong and steady and true.

Like Quint himself.

She didn't know when she'd fallen in love with him. Her battered hero. Maybe a little bit when he'd automatically rushed to save Hannah from harm and then passed out cold on the hospital floor at the sight of a needle. And maybe a little more when he'd looked so sheepish about rescuing Barney.

Even when he'd thought he could use her to come between Fern and his grandfather, he'd been unable to avoid coming to her rescue. Not because he loved her, but because he was good and kind and brave.

The kind of man who rescued cats.

Tears laced her silent laughter.

He hadn't said he loved her. She refused to admit he might not. She wouldn't let him not love her.

Her family could tell him how stubborn she could be.

She watched him sleep. Dark stubble shadowed the lower

half of his face. She'd never noticed how dark his lashes were as they rested against his lightly tanned face. Or how long. He breathed noisily through slightly parted lips.

Lips she wanted to kiss.

Everyone else had gone to supper. She couldn't eat.

Their children would be little terrors. How could they not be with two such stubborn people for parents?

The white hospital linen made his hair look even blacker.

What color would their children's eyes be? Washed-out blue like hers or ever-changing shades of green like Quint's? Possibly a mixture of the two. Turquoise. She'd always liked turquoise.

Quint's leg ached and a few other parts smarted. Where was she? With the nurse's help he'd washed, shaved and brushed his teeth. He'd turned down a pain pill. His mind had to stay clear. Focused. The clock on the wall read almost 10:00 a.m.

Had he chased her away already? He couldn't remember what had been said yesterday. He only remembered she'd been there once when he'd opened his eyes.

If she'd told him she loved him, he'd remember that.

She'd said she was getting married. He reached deep inside himself for joy. Nothing. Who was she marrying? Had she said? She couldn't marry anyone but him.

Footsteps. Voices. His heart sped up.

He managed to smile as his mother, grandfather and Phil walked in. They talked, and he halfway listened while his ears strained to hear other footsteps. His visitors didn't mention Greeley. He lacked the courage to ask.

Phil looked past Quint's bed and his eyeballs practically bulged out. Quint started grinning before he turned his head.

A huge metal shield-like sculpture walked into the room on a pair of dynamite legs that ended in red shoes. Not any red shoes, but shoes with high heels and hundreds of thin straps. They were the sexiest pair of shoes Quint had ever seen.

Mary Lassiter followed the artwork. A babble of conversation broke out, but Quint ignored it, intent on the person carrying the wall sculpture.

Greeley propped the sculpture against the far wall where Quint could see it. Every line of her body told him she knew he was watching her. Swiveling around she gave him a fixed smile. Starting with her red-painted toes, Quint greedily drank in the sight of her. Phil's eyeballs must have popped out by now. There wasn't enough material in her short-sleeved, thigh-high red dress to make a handkerchief.

She'd never bore him.

His gaze returned to the artwork. "A Greeley Lassiter sculpture," he murmured.

"Do you like it?"

A simple question asked in a carefully casual voice. The anxiety in her eyes told Quint the answer was not simple. He had to get it right. Closing his eyes halfway, he studied the sculpture, carefully moving his head on the pillow to gain perspective.

Her sculptures were like her. Superficially sleek and polished with an in-your-face attitude. One had to look beyond the surface into the depths where subtle, complex emotions darted and swirled, one moment visible, the next hidden. Powerful emotions that told a story—and gripped your gut.

This wasn't the sculpture he'd commissioned for his grandfather.

As Quint stared at the sculpture, the swirling images coalesced and parted only to merge again. And to him it read like an open book. Dazzling him.

He couldn't begin to comprehend how she did it. With nothing but scrap metal she'd portrayed tiny moments of his life. A car key, Barney wagging his tail, teenagers running down an athletic field, a child in a wheelchair with a dog beside her, Hannah and her butterfly, Santa Claus driving a truck. Letters in assorted sizes had been riveted to the sculpture. Nonsense letters, they spelled no words.

Unless one rearranged them. Maybe he was still hungover from the pain medication, but Quint couldn't seem to arrange the letters to spell anything but, ''The Hero.''

She'd created a medal for him.

Looking at her, Quint shook his head, struggling to maintain his composure. They were always shoving pills down his throat. Didn't they know medicine made a man emotional? If he spoke, he'd bawl like a baby.

Her face went very still.

He cleared his throat, forcing himself to tell her the truth. ''I'm not a hero. Warren was right behind me. If he'd been ahead of me, he'd have pulled out the kids. If I'd stopped to think of the danger, I wouldn't have done it. I sure wouldn't have gone back for Suzie if I'd known she was a cat or known this would happen.'' He gestured toward his leg.

''I finished the sculpture before I heard about the accident and your injury.''

''I don't get it.'' Why would she call him a hero when he hadn't done anything?

She laughed at his obvious confusion, and in her laughter he saw love and acceptance. At that second the significance of the key hit him. It had nothing to do with the trucking company or his sports car, but had everything to do with their banter at the party when he'd asked her if the key on her jewelry was the key to her heart and she'd informed him her heart wasn't that easily accessed.

''The key to your heart,'' he said, knowing it was much more. The key to all her secrets. He held out his hand, and when she gave him hers, he drew her closer to the bed. ''I'll take very good care of it.'' He meant more than the sculpture.

''I know you will. You're the kind of man who takes excellent care of everyone who touches your life.'' She pressed her palm to his face. ''That's why you're my hero and why I love you.''

Quint tugged at her hand, pulling her down to where he

could kiss her. Considering the circumstances, it was a very satisfactory kiss.

When he finally lifted his head, he heard his grandfather telling everyone he was counting the days until he could hold his great-grandchildren. The pink patches on Greeley's cheeks said she'd heard Big Ed, too.

Squeezing her hand, Quint said, "I don't care who you marry as long as it's me."

He looked at her mother and asked in a firm voice which quieted the entire room, "Mary, may I marry your youngest daughter?"

Mary pretended to give him a stern look. "I think you'd better. If you don't, Worth will come after you with Grandpa Yancy's shotgun."

A babble of congratulations broke out. Quint grinned at Greeley. "I guess that settles that. I'm not exactly in any condition to outrun your brother."

The harsh hospital light glinted off the moisture in her eyes, and she ducked her head. A single tear fell to his sheet.

Alarmed, Quint reached up and touched her cheek. "What did I say? Did I do it wrong? I didn't tell you I love you, did I? I do love you. I want to spend the rest of my life loving you, learning all your secrets."

She blinked her eyes rapidly and said in a shaky voice, "You didn't call me Mom's stepdaughter, and you didn't call Worth my half-brother."

Quint didn't mind one bit the way she clung to his hand. "I may be a slow learner," he said, "but I know who your real family is, and I know who your real mother is."

He didn't want to think about how short her dress was when she bent over the bed to kiss him. After a second, he didn't.

Later, when everyone else had gone, Quint couldn't resist asking, "Are you going to wear a red wedding dress?"

"Of course not," she said indignantly.

"I can hardly wait to see what you wear on our wedding night."

A delightful flush ran up her neck. "I'm sure I'll wear the kind of thing all brides wear." Greeley's gaze skittered past him.

She'd wear red.

She wouldn't wear it long.

EPILOGUE

SEVERAL MONTHS LATER Greeley drove her cherry-red sports car from the garage at the Double Nickel into the bright September afternoon. High on the distant slopes of Mt. Sopris, patches of aspen shone gold under an impossibly blue sky. Sunlight glinted off Greeley's left hand. "Happy the bride," she thought contentedly, knowing a full-scale blizzard couldn't have ruined her day.

"Stop the car a second, will you?"

They screeched to a halt under the log arch of the ranch gate as Greeley hit the brakes. "What's wrong? Is your leg bothering you?" Guilt flooded her. "Instead of driving, we should have gone on a cruise or to Thomas's hotel on St. Bart's. You could have stretched out in the sun and recuperated."

He waved off her concern. "My leg is fine, and I am fully recuperated." He'd been determined to walk to the altar under his own power and with no discernible limp. "I wanted to stop at the sign." He nodded toward the weathered strip of wood. "Hope Valley. The first time I came to the ranch, I read that and sneered." He added wryly, "I was a fool. What if I hadn't come?"

The question brought a moment of stark terror, and she wanted to leap across the car into his arms to reassure herself he was really there. He thought he'd stormed the walls and won the key to her heart, but she knew the real prize belonged to her. A man who loved her in spite of her flaws and background. His love warmed her, wrapped protectively around her, made her life complete.

"I've been meaning to ask you who put up the sign, but I've been distracted a lot lately." Quint trailed a lazy finger up her arm, sending exquisite sensations shimmering over her skin.

Greeley took a deep breath and concentrated on answering his question. "Jacob Nichol settled the area and called the ranch the Double Nickel after himself and his wife, Anna. Anna's the one who named this Hope Valley. She and Jacob moved from back East to start their married life here, and Anna felt hopeful about their future."

Quint lightly caressed the back of her neck. "Like us."

A hummingbird whistled past the open car window, and a small, secret door kept securely locked within Greeley suddenly swung open to admit glorious light. "Yes," she half whispered, "like us. Like me. Thank you."

"You're welcome. For anything in particular?"

"For not driving my car to the wedding so we had to come back here to switch cars. And for wanting to stop at this sign."

Quint gave her a quizzical look. "I have the feeling you're somehow referring to more than worry about someone spraying shoe polish on your new car during our wedding luncheon."

"Jacob and Anna were Mom's great-grandparents, so they weren't related to me. Beau was an orphan, and I know nothing of Fern's ancestors, so I had to borrow Mom's family history. I've always hated that Jacob and Anna weren't really mine, because I admired Anna's courage so much." Greeley blinked away a tear. "I wanted to be connected to her, and suddenly I am."

Quint looked confused. She gave him a tremulous smile. "What you said about us being like them. It's crazy, but it's as if Anna's somehow part of me now. In my mind. Telling me how she felt when she painted that sign."

His hand cupped her cheek. "How did she feel?"

Greeley leaned into his warm palm. "Thankful for Jacob's love. Filled with wonder and joy that he wanted to share his life with her. Brimming with love. And unable to find the words to express to him all the emotions overflowing her heart.''

Quint's hand tightened, and she watched the play of muscles across his face. ''Maybe he saw what was in her heart,'' he said softly. ''And felt the same.'' He wiped a solitary tear from Greeley's face, then cleared his throat and added with suspicious blandness, ''And to show her how much he loved her, he probably bought her her own mule.''

''Mule!'' Greeley grabbed the front of his shirt and tugged. He came willingly. ''Are you calling my lovely sports car a mule?'' she asked indignantly.

Quint's laughter spilled from the car.

And into her mouth when she pulled off their sunglasses and kissed him. Her fingers tightened around a fistful of shirt fabric. He gave off incredible heat, warming every part of her body. Without touching her. Except for his lips. And his tongue. She wanted to rip off his clothes.

Quint loosened her grasp on his shirt, and straightened up. ''I think you'd better wait until we get to a hotel, Mrs. Damian, before you continue demonstrating your appreciation.'' His voice deepened. ''The sooner we get there, the better.'' A small grin loaded with sexy male arrogance lurked at the corners of his mouth.

Greeley's insides dipped and swayed, but she managed to say casually, as if it didn't matter to her, ''We could probably find a vacant room in Glenwood Springs. It's less than fifty miles downvalley.''

''I thought maybe we could go back to Aspen and sneak through the back door of the St. Christopher Hotel without anyone seeing us.''

Laughing at his plaintive voice, she turned the key in the car's ignition. ''If Worth saw us come back, he'd have heart failure, sure you'd changed your mind and he wasn't getting rid of me after all.''

Quint settled back in the passenger seat. ''Good thing I'm an old married man, or I'd be jealous of your brother. At lunch the women were flocking around him like bees around honey."

Greeley pointed her car toward the highway. "Women are always flocking around him. Worth's one of the most eligible bachelors in the area, but he says he'll never get married. He claims having three sisters has taught him women are crazy and any man stupid enough to get tangled up with one gets what he deserves."

"Poor slob. That's the kind of boast a man makes just before he goes down for the count. Look at me."

It was impossible to take exception to Quint's last statement when he delivered it with such smug satisfaction.

The last rays of the setting sun poured into the hotel suite in Glenwood Springs, setting aglow the red nightgown and robe thrown on a chair across the room. Quint propped his head on his hand and watched his wife sleep. A sheet barely covered Greeley's more interesting parts. Resisting the urge to remove it, he turned his gaze to the long, bare legs entwined with his.

When he thought how easily, through his own stubbornness and stupidity, he could have missed knowing this incredible happiness, he felt remarkably lucky. And blessed.

And to think he had Fern Kelly to thank. Greeley had changed her mind a million times about whether to invite Fern to the wedding. She'd finally sent word through Cheyenne's movie-star friend, but Fern hadn't responded. Nobody missed her.

Including Greeley, Quint had been pleased to note.

Her family had been there celebrating with them. And his. Soon he and Greeley would start to build their family. He pictured her large with his child. She'd be beautiful.

Greeley rolled over, curling into his body. The scent of wildflowers teased his nostrils. Her breath warmed his skin. In moving, she'd dislodged the sheet. He wanted to run his hands down her slim, soft body, and turn drowsiness into desire. Watch her lovely eyes as they filled with a sexy, feminine awareness. Because he loved her, Quint let her sleep.

A warm, moist tongue curled around his nipple.

He swallowed a startled chuckle. Two could play her game. Laying his palm on her hip, Quint smiled when he heard a quick, indrawn breath.

Her next move wiped the smile off his face. His body tensed and hardened. "The hands of an artist," he muttered, and flipped her on her back.

Greeley's eyes laughed up at him. "We're supposed to be spending ten days driving wherever the mood and roads take us. We'll never be able to explain why we never made it any further than Glenwood Springs for the first three days of our honeymoon."

Quint drew circles of ever-decreasing size around her breast. "I don't think we'll have to explain why to anyone." The tip hardened, enticing his lips. "And today's the fourth day, not the third," he murmured against warm flesh.

Her legs moved restlessly against the sheets. "We could say the hot spring pools were good therapy for your leg. If we ever go near them."

Her expressive eyes aroused him as much as her ragged breathing and lovely body. Her softness. Her acceptance. Quint slid his hand downward, heady with the knowledge of the secrets he'd already learned about her, eager to learn more. "Heat therapy is wonderful medicine," he said solemnly. "I feel very good." He caressed her intimately. "And very hot."

Greeley gave a strangled choke of laughter and welcomed him as he slid deeply into her.

Afterwards she lay sprawled across him, her head on his chest. "I suppose you think I like that better than driving my new car," she grumbled.

He pretended to consider the question. "I figure it's a toss up," he said at last.

She scowled in mock ferocity. "The only reason you

bought me that car is so you wouldn't have to share your car.''

He'd been lucky to find the thirty-year-old classic sports car in fairly good condition. The fellows at the terminal hadn't minded a little overtime helping Quint get the car into near-mint condition for Greeley's wedding present. ''I bought it because I like you in red.''

''Liar. You haven't let me be in anything red almost from the moment we hit this hotel.''

Quint framed her face with his hands, drinking in her singular beauty. The determined chin. The slightest hint of vulnerability he knew she'd never completely conquer. The generous, smiling, passionate mouth.

And he knew, more precious than any medal or trophy he'd ever win was the love in her fabulous eyes.

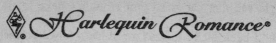

Harlequin Romance® is proud to announce the birth of some very special new arrivals in:

Because two's company and three (or more) is a family!

Our bouncing-babies series is back! Throughout 2000 we'll be delivering more bundles of joy, and introducing their brave moms and dads as they experience the thrills—and spills!—of parenthood!

Our first adorable addition is due in February 2000:

THE BILLIONAIRE DADDY
by **Renee Roszel**

Look out for other BABY BOOM romances from more of your favorite authors throughout 2000.

Available wherever Harlequin books are sold.

HARLEQUIN®
Makes any time special.™

Visit us at: www.romance.net

HRBB

If you enjoyed what you just read,
then we've got an offer you can't resist!

Take 2 bestselling love stories FREE!

Plus get a FREE surprise gift!

Clip this page and mail it to Harlequin Reader Service®

IN U.S.A.	IN CANADA
3010 Walden Ave.	P.O. Box 609
P.O. Box 1867	Fort Erie, Ontario
Buffalo, N.Y. 14240-1867	L2A 5X3

YES! Please send me 2 free Harlequin Romance® novels and my free surprise gift. Then send me 4 brand-new novels every month, which I will receive months before they're available in stores. In the U.S.A., bill me at the bargain price of $2.90 plus 25¢ delivery per book and applicable sales tax, if any*. In Canada, bill me at the bargain price of $3.34 plus 25¢ delivery per book and applicable taxes**. That's the complete price and a savings of over 10% off the cover prices—what a great deal! I understand that accepting the 2 free books and gift places me under no obligation ever to buy any books. I can always return a shipment and cancel at any time. Even if I never buy another book from Harlequin, the 2 free books and gift are mine to keep forever. So why not take us up on our invitation. You'll be glad you did!

116 HEN CNEP
316 HEN CNEQ

_____
Name   (PLEASE PRINT)

_____
Address   Apt.#

_____
City   State/Prov.   Zip/Postal Code

* Terms and prices subject to change without notice. Sales tax applicable in N.Y.
** Canadian residents will be charged applicable provincial taxes and GST.
   All orders subject to approval. Offer limited to one per household.
   ® are registered trademarks of Harlequin Enterprises Limited.

HROM99   ©1998 Harlequin Enterprises Limited

Three compelling novels
by award-winning writer

KAREN YOUNG

HEAT
of the
NIGHT

**Three dramatic stories of the risks men and
women take to protect their children.**

Debt of Love—Tyler Madison and Alexandra Tate are
drawn together by the urgent need to help Tyler's nephew
after a devastating accident.

Touch the Dawn—Mitchell St. Cyr flees with his children
to protect them from their stepfather and finds haven with
his friends until he learns that their daughter Jacky is a
county juvenile officer.

The Silence of Midnight—When his son is kidnapped,
Sheriff Jake McAdam feels he's failed—as a lawman, a
husband, *a father*.

On sale December 1999 at your favorite retail outlet.

HARLEQUIN®
Makes any time special ™

Visit us at www.romance.net

PSBR3100

WHO'S AFRAID OF THE BIG BAD WOLFE?

Certainly not you—not when the Wolfe
happens to be a sexy, dynamic lawman!
Pick up

And meet two of the Wolfe brothers,
who know all the laws of seduction
and romance.

Joan Hohl, one of Silhouette's bestselling
authors, has thrilled readers with her Wolfe family
saga. Don't miss this special two-book collection
featuring the first two Big Bad Wolfe stories.

Look for *Big Bad Wolfe: Ready To Wed?*
on sale in December 1999.

Available at your favorite retail outlet.

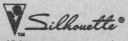

Visit us at www.romance.net   PSBR2100

3 Stories of Holiday Romance from three
bestselling Harlequin® authors

*Valentine
Babies*

by

ANNE
STUART

TARA TAYLOR
QUINN

JULE
McBRIDE

Goddess in Waiting by Anne Stuart
Edward walks into Marika's funky maternity shop to pick
up some things for his sister. He doesn't expect to assist
in the delivery of a baby and fall for outrageous Marika.

Gabe's Special Delivery by Tara Taylor Quinn
On February 14, Gabe Stone finds a living, breathing
valentine on his doorstep—his daughter. Her mother
has given Gabe four hours to adjust to fatherhood,
resolve custody and win back his ex-wife?

My Man Valentine by Jule McBride
Everyone knows Eloise Hunter and C. D. Valentine
are in love. Except Eloise and C. D. Then, one of
Eloise's baby-sitting clients leaves her with a baby to
mind, and C. D. swings into protector mode.

VALENTINE BABIES
On sale January 2000 at your favorite retail outlet.

◈ HARLEQUIN®
Makes any time special ™

Visit us at www.romance.net   PHVALB